LIBE

א

VEL

CXI

LIBER ALEPH VEL CXI

The BOOK *of* WISDOM *or* FOLLY

in the Form of an Epistle of
666
THE GREAT WILD BEAST
to his Son
777

being
THE EQUINOX
VOLUME III NUMBER VI

by
THE MASTER THERION
(Aleister Crowley)

Anno IIIxxi Sol in 0° Aries
March 20, 1991 E.V. 10:02 P.M. E.S.T.

SAMUEL WEISER, INC.
York Beach, Maine

First published in 1991 by
Samuel Weiser, Inc.
Box 612
York Beach, Maine 03910

Second printing, 1992

First edition published in 1962 by
Thelema Publishing Co., West Point, California

Library of Congress Cataloging-in-Publication Data

Crowley, Aleister, 1875-1947.
Liber aleph vel CXI: the book of wisdom or folly / Aleister Crowley
p. cm.
1. Occultism. 2. Spiritual life. 3. Meditations. I. Title
BF 1999.C743 1991
133--dc20 91-8023
CIP

ISBN 0-87728-729-5
ISSN 1050-2904
MG

Printed in the United States of America.

The paper used in this publication meets the minimum requirements of the American National Standard for Permanence of Paper for Printed Library Materials Z39.48-1984

Table of Contents

Introduction
to the First Edition

HIS BOOK HAS HAD A STRANGE FATE. IT IS ONE of the masterworks of the late Aleister Crowley, completed at the end of the First World War, in March of 1918, when the Central Powers were crumbling. On several occasions it was attempted to publish it; twice before it was actually set to print. The last time, the printing was completed in England, but the author's death on December 1st of 1947 intervened, and the edition was not issued.

This is one of Crowley's greatest and deepest books, into which he put his very blood. There is no better way to show the why and how the book was written than to let the author explain it himself. We quote from his as yet unpublished *Confessions*:*

> *Liber Aleph, the Book of Wisdom or Folly*, was intended to express the heart of my doctrine in the most deep and delicate dimensions. It is the most tense and intense book that I have ever composed. The thought is so concentrated and, if I may use the word, nervous, that both to write then, and to read now, involved and involves an almost intolerable strain. I remember how I used to sit at my desk night after night — it was the bitterest winter that had been known in New York for many years, but even if the central heating had been the flames of hell itself, I doubt whether I should have been warm. Night after night I sat, all through, rigid as a corpse, and icier; the whole of my life concentrated in two spots: the small section of my brain which was occupied in the work, and my right wrist and fingers. I remember with absolute clearness that my consciousness appeared to start from a perfectly dead forearm.

---

* NOTE TO SECOND EDITION: Parts I and II were published in 1929 by the Mandrake Press in London. Parts I-VI were published as *The Confessions of Aleister Crowley*, ed. John Symonds and Kenneth Grant (London: Jonathan Cape, and New York: Hill & Wang, 1969); the quotation is from pp. 831-2. Herinafter cited as Crowley, *Confessions*.

> The book is written in prose, yet there is a formal circumscription more imminent than anything which would have been possible in poetry. I limited myself by making a point of dealing thoroughly with a given subject in a single page. It was an acute agony, similar to that of Asana, to write, and the effort removed me so far from normal human consciousness that there was something indicibly ghastly in its unnaturalness when I got into bed in full daylight in the hope of acquiring a particle of warmth from the complacent "Camel."

When he began writing *Liber Aleph*, Crowley thought he was addressing it to his magical "son" O.I.V.V.I.O., whom he then believed would be the child prophesied in *The Book of the Law*. In several ways he strove to help this "son" in his progress. Thereby he was fulfilling the very prophecy in the Book:

> It shall be his child & that strangely. Let him not seek after this; for thereby alone can he fall from it. [*AL* III:47]

Up to 1919, events allowed Crowley to persist in his belief that O.I.V.V.I.O. would be the "child" promised in *AL* (although in the Samadhic writing of *Liber Aleph* itself he had foreseen — see Chapter 166 — the Truth of this matter). From then on, things began to happen that forced Crowley to become doubtful against his every wish and hope. By 1924 it became conclusive that O.I.V.V.I.O. (motto of the "son" on assuming the grade of Magister Templi) had failed to annihilate the personality completely.

But what mattered this to the Secret Chiefs, who spun their web about the Scribe so that, motivated by all the wealth of love in his nature, he should strain in this mighty effort? For, in one sense, *Liber Aleph* is addressed to the child of The Great Wild Beast, and the child of Man is mankind; and in another sense, the child promised in *AL* shall yet arise — in its own good time.

Therefore, for that child, and its brothers and sisters everywhere, we are now issuing this Work at a time when the sense of frustration in all continents of the globe has led almost to a vision of complete Chaos.

THE EDITORS

Prolegomenon
to the Second Edition

And I gave my heart to know wisdom, and to know madness
and folly: I perceived that this also is vexation of spirit.
— Ecclesiastes

Do what thou wilt shall be the whole of the Law.

LEISTER CROWLEY'S GREAT GIFT WAS HIS ABILITY to voice truths that most are fortunate to symbolize, if indeed envision at all. In the two hundred and eight chapters of *Liber Aleph* he sets out an impressive array of spiritual concepts. It is an educational treatise in the purest sense, that of the transmission of hard-won wisdom from generation to generation.

Crowley wrote *Liber Aleph* with a self-imposed mental and physical discipline that discouraged digression; in the holograph manuscript, with but few exceptions, each subject exactly fills its chapter, and each chapter its page. Yet there is a wondrous continuity as he turns from one subject to the next, pouring out his encyclopedic knowledge. The Holy Qabalah, Magick, the psychology of dreams and the unconscious, the formulæ of initiation, the education of children and the training of disciples, the mystical trances, drugs, sex, love and death; these are but a few of the topics treated, not in passing, but in profound depth.

In later life Crowley would turn to *Liber Aleph* again and again, quoting entire chapters to elucidate a principle, or referring serious readers to the book for a full treatment of a particular topic. It is as if, having once expressed himself so well and at such great cost, he was unwilling or unable to improve on his expression. It is possibly Crowley's most comprehensive exposition of his mature magical philosophy.

Liber Aleph is deliberately couched in an archaic, epistolatory style strangely suited to the book's many difficult subjects. But what would be quaint affectation in the hands of another writer effectively elevates the language to the dignity of the author's thought. Curiously, this formalism also helps sustain an undercurrent of emotion that is nothing, more or less, than the love of a father for his son.

Crowley described *Liber Aleph* as "an extended and elaborate commentary on *The Book of the Law*, in the form of a letter from the Master Therion to his magical son."[1] In this last respect it resembles another book of magical instruction, *The Book of the Sacred Magic of Abramelin the Mage as Delivered by Abraham the Jew unto his Son Lamech*, whose English translator was S. L. Mathers, a cofounder of the Hermetic Order of the Golden Dawn.[2] Crowley was initiated into the Golden Dawn in 1898, at the age of 23, and received his earliest magical training there. While mere psychobiography is a sure route to misunderstanding Crowley, Mathers was one of his few "father figures," and *Abramelin* a work he studied and practiced intensely in his youth. Although *Liber Aleph* was written almost twenty years later and half a world away, the events, personalities and concepts that occasioned its creation have their roots in Crowley's early life. It is to this period that we must turn for an understanding of its genesis.

In 1900 a membership rebellion sundered the Golden Dawn, and Crowley interrupted his practice of the Abramelin magical system to stand by his embattled leader Mathers. By 1903 the Order was in open schism, but Crowley had since retired from magical practice to study yoga and immerse himself in travel, sport and poetry. That August he married Rose Edith Kelly. She had little interest in magick and less knowledge, but was to lead her husband on a spiritual adventure that would shape the course of his life.

In early 1904, while returning to England from a belated honeymoon in Ceylon, the Crowleys impulsively disembarked at Cairo for an extended stay. Crowley performed a magical invocation for Rose's amusement, and she became strangely inspired for several weeks, informing her baffled husband that "they are waiting for you," and "it's all about the child." By careful questioning, Crowley determined that the "waiter" was the Egyptian god Horus. Rose instructed him to enter his

---

[1] [Crowley], "Curriculum of A∴A∴," *The Equinox* III(1) (Detroit: Universal, 1919; reprinted New York: Samuel Weiser, 1972), p. 27.

[2] [Abraham ben Simeon], *The Sacred Magic of Abramelin the Mage*, trans. S. L. Mathers (London: Watkins, 1898).

temple at exactly noon on three successive days and write down what he heard. He reluctantly complied, and on April 8, 9, and 10 received a voice dictation from an entity he later described as a "præter-human intelligence" named Aiwaz (or Aiwass). This was *The Book of the Law*, formally titled *Liber L vel Legis sub figura CCXX* (hereinafter cited as *Liber Legis*).

Crowley's innate skepticism led him to doubt *Liber Legis*; force of circumstance eventually convinced him that the book was profoundly prophetic, containing irrefutable internal evidence of its authenticity, "concealing in cipher propositions unknown to me, majestic and profound; foretelling events public and private beyond my control, or that of any man."[3] It was several years before Crowley accepted *Liber Legis* for what it was and is: the founding document of a New Æon of which he was prophet and Magus.

After receiving *Liber Legis*, Crowley began work to establish a new Order — the A∴A∴ — with the avowed aim of placing initiation on a scientific basis in accord with the principles of the New Æon. He taught that the A∴A∴ is ultimately governed by the Secret Chiefs, the Great White Brotherhood that guides human evolution. It is the new expression of the initiatory current that had informed its precursors, the Theosophical Society and the Golden Dawn. Crowley was thus a successor to Madame Blavatsky, and continued her work of synthesizing the mystery traditions of East and West. He also succeeded S. L. Mathers as Chief Adept, and purified the Golden Dawn system in the light of *Liber Legis*. This new system was largely codified by 1909, when it began accepting members.

Members of the Golden Dawn (and its inner order *Rosae Rubeae et Aureae Crucis*) worked through a sequence of grades that correspond to the sephiroth of the Qabalistic Tree of Life. This is true of the A∴A∴ system as well, where a novitiate grade of Probationer ($0^\circ=0^\square$) leads to a series of grades from Malkuth (Neophyte $1^\circ=10^\square$) through Chesed (Exempt Adept $7^\circ=4^\square$).

The highest A∴A∴ grades are those of the Third Order, the S∴S∴, which correspond to the sephiroth Binah (Magister Templi $8^\circ=3^\square$), Chokmah (Magus $9^\circ=2^\square$) and Kether (Ipsissimus $10^\circ=1^\square$). To proceed to these grades, the Exempt Adept $7^\circ=4^\square$ must first take the Oath of the Abyss, in which he swears to

3 [Crowley], *The Equinox of the Gods* (*The Equinox* III(3), London: O.T.O., 1936), pp. 104-5.

interpret all phenomena as a direct dealing of God with his soul. The adept then becomes a Babe of the Abyss, and either fails to annihilate the personality and becomes a Black Brother (see chapter 104), or successfully attains the grade of Magister Templi $8^\circ = 3^\square$, becoming a Master of the Temple. Of this grade, Crowley writes:

> In *The Vision and the Voice*,[4] the attainment of the grade of Master of the Temple was symbolized by the adept pouring every drop of his blood, that is his whole individual life, into the Cup of the Scarlet Woman, who represents Universal Impersonal Life. There remains ... of the adept "nothing but a little pile of dust."[5]

A.'.A.'. tradition holds that any aspirant may take the Oath of the Abyss, but to do so without completing the balancing and perfecting work required in the intervening grades is to court disaster. Unresolved personality complexes resist the annihilation of the ego, and the result — what might be characterized as ontological solipsism — can lead to mania and madness.

Crowley describes the grade above Magister Templi, that of Magus $9^\circ = 2^\square$, as follows:

> Just as the Master of the Temple is sworn to interpret every phenomenon as a particular dealing of God with his soul, so is the Magus to make his every act an expression of his magical formula.[6]

> The essential characteristic of the Grade is that its possessor utters a Creative Magical Word, which transforms the planet on which he lives by the installation of new officers to preside over its initiation. This can take place only at an "Equinox of the Gods" at the end of an "Æon"; that is, when the secret formula which expresses the Law of its action becomes outworn and useless to its further development.... A Magus can therefore only appear as such to the world at intervals of some centuries; accounts of historical Magi, and their Words, are given in *Liber Aleph*.[7]

Crowley's name as Magus $9^\circ = 2^\square$ was ΤΟ ΜΕΓΑ ΘΗΡΙΟΝ, or The Master Therion. Its literal translation is "the Great Beast," and it adds to 666 in Greek numeration. Like Lao-tse, Buddha, Krishna, Mohammed and other Magi of the past (see chapters 68-74), the Master Therion uttered his Word, inaugurating the New Æon of Horus that commenced in 1904 with the reception of *Liber Legis*. Crowley puts this in an historical perspective by

4 [Crowley], "Liber CDXVII, The Vision and the Voice," in *The Equinox* I(5), London, 1911, supplement. *The Equinox* I(1-10) was reprinted in 1972 by Samuel Weiser, New York.

5 Crowley, *Confessions*, p. 795.

6 *Ibid.*, p. 800.

7 [Crowley], "One Star in Sight," *Magick in Theory and Practice* (*Book IV*, *Part III*) (Paris and London: privately printed, 1929-30; numerous reprints), pp. 234-5.

describing past, present and future Æons, and the magical formulæ that govern the evolution of consciousness:

> The Hierarchy of the Egyptians gives us this genealogy; Isis, Osiris, Horus. Now the "pagan" period is that of Isis; a pastoral, natural period of simple magic. Next with Buddha, Christ, and others there came in the Equinox of Osiris; when sorrow and death are the principal objects of man's thought, and his magical formula is that of sacrifice. Now, with Mohammed perhaps as its forerunner, comes in the Equinox of Horus, the young child who rises strong and conquering (with his twin Harpocrates) to avenge Osiris, and bring on the age of strength and splendour. His formula is not yet fully understood. Following him will arise the Equinox of Ma, the Goddess of Justice, it may be a hundred or ten thousand years from now; for the Computation of Time is not here as There.[8]

Astrological Ages depend upon the gradual precession of the equinoxes. According to astronomical observation and measurement, the zodiacal sign on the horizon at dawn on the spring equinox changes approximately every 2,156 years. These Ages are not necessarily coterminous with Æons, which may vary in length. But while the inauguration of the Age of Aquarius coincided with the inception of the Æon of Horus, their relationship is not immediately obvious. Horus is the "crowned and conquering child," and his Æon is characterized by "force and fire." These are not qualities traditionally associated with the humanistic sign Aquarius, but they are typical of its zodiacal opposite, Leo. Crowley explains that:

> To talk of the Ages of Pisces and Aquarius is incomplete. The Age has also the opposite sign as one of its characteristics, and this may at times be even stronger than the original sign. To call this the Aquarian Age is really a joke. The characteristic so far has been much more that of Leo.[9]

The reception of *The Book of the Law* was effected through the agency of Rose Edith Crowley, who was the first Scarlet Woman, or magical consort, of the Beast. Of the Beast and the Scarlet Woman, Crowley wrote:

---

[8] Crowley, Old Comment to *Liber Legis* III:34, first published in *The Equinox* I(7), London, 1912, p. 387. Crowley's "old" and "new" commentaries to *Liber Legis* appear together in Crowley, *Magical and Philosophical Commentaries on the Book of the Law*, ed. John Symonds and Kenneth Grant (Montréal: 93 Publishing, 1974). Many commentaries only appear in this edition; an abridged edition is Crowley, *The Law is for All*, ed. Israel Regardie (St. Paul: Llewellyn, 1975, reprinted Scottsdale, AZ: New Falcon Publications, 1991). Commentaries are hereinafter cited by chapter and verse of *Liber Legis*.

[9] Crowley, letter to W. B. Crow, 11 November 1944.

The Beast and the Scarlet Woman are avatars of Tao and Teh, Shiva and Shakti.... The Beast appears to be a definite individual: to wit, the man Aleister Crowley. But the Scarlet Woman is an officer replacable as need arises.[10]

Crowley's spiritual progress from Magister Templi 8°=3▫ to Magus 9°=2▫ spanned the period 1914 to 1919, corresponding closely with his sojourn in the United States. It was assisted over the years by a series of women, whom he likened to officers in the ceremony of his initiation. Most if not all were his lovers, and as magical catalysts they had theriomorphic names: "The Cat," "The Snake," "The Dog," "The Owl," "The Monkey," "The Camel" and "The Dragon." They are discussed in chapter 176 of the present work.[11]

Three of these "officers" had roles in the creation of *Liber Aleph*. "The Cat" was Jeanne Foster (Soror Hilarion); her central role is discussed below. Her successor, "The Camel," was Roddie Minor (Soror Ahitha), with whom Crowley lived when he wrote the work. She was briefly succeeded by "The Dragon," Marie Lavroff Rohling (Soror Olun); Crowley became involved with her during its composition (see chapters 101-102 and 109-110). All three of these women were Scarlet Women in their turn, and all eventually fell away from the role.[12] Soror Ahitha failed "from indifference to the Work." Although Crowley later considered Soror Olun "a doubtful case," he credited her with helping to inspire the writing of *Liber Aleph*; she failed "from indecision." But we are especially concerned here with the earliest of these Scarlet Women, Jeanne Foster. Although her association with the Beast was fleeting, it was she who unknowingly occasioned the writing of *Liber Aleph*.

Jeanne Robert Foster (*neé* Olivier, 1884-1970) was one of Crowley's great loves. She escaped from small town life in upstate New York by marrying an man older than her father. They settled in New York City, where she became a poetess and assistant editor of the *Review of Reviews*.[13] She met Crowley, who was

---

[10] Crowley, New Comment to *Liber Legis* I:15.

[11] This important period of Crowley's life is discussed fully in "Liber LXXIII, The Urn," published as Chapters 81-87 of his *Confessions*.

[12] The quotations following are from Crowley's summary of Scarlet Women as of 1921, published in his New Comment to *Liber Legis*, I:15.

[13] William M. Murphy, *Prodigal Father: The Life of John Butler Yeats* (Cornell UP, Ithaca and London, 1979), p. 395.

then writing for *Vanity Fair*, in June of 1915 at a party given by a journalist. It was love at first sight; Crowley wrote that "I saw my ideal incarnate ... I really loved her with a love more exalted than aught in all my experience."[14] She kept him waiting a month before consummating the liaison, probably something of a record for Crowley, who wrote in his *Confessions*: "I endured the torture of absence, of doubt, of despair, with all the might of my manhood."[14]

It was indeed a serious relationship; they wrote love poetry to one another, and she considered divorcing her husband to marry Crowley, who longed to have a child with her. Jeanne assumed the office of Scarlet Woman in his magical workings, choosing Hilarion as her mystic name. In late September Crowley tried to beget a child by her and — as evidenced in the final poems of *The Golden Rose* (the unpublished sonnet cycle chronicling their affair) — he believed he had succeeded.

In early October Crowley set out for a tour of the West Coast, followed by Jeanne, who had "decided to spice the romance and adventure by taking her husband in tow."[15] They took a side trip to Vancouver, where Crowley visited Charles Stansfeld Jones, a member of the A.'.A.'. and the Ordo Templi Orientis (O.T.O.). They parted in California; on Crowley's return to New York he learned that she had dropped him. He felt the loss acutely. He had been certain she had conceived his child, later writing that "I did not know that I was attempting a physical impossibility."[16]

Crowley regained his emotional equilibrium, dismissing the affair as an illusion, and Jeanne Foster as deceitful. He decided that she had "failed from respectability" in her role as Scarlet Woman. But five years later he would write: "I have not been in love since 1915.... Did she really 'break my heart'?"[16]

Events took a strange turn the following year. In the summer of 1916, Crowley received a telegram from Vancouver informing him that Charles Stansfeld Jones, Frater Achad, a Neophyte $1^{\circ}=10^{\square}$ of A.'.A.'., had taken the Oath of the Abyss and emerged a Master of the Temple $8^{\circ}=3^{\square}$. It seemed that Therion and Hilarion had produced a child after all, a 777 to Therion's 666.

[14] Crowley, *Confessions*, pp. 798-9.

[15] *Ibid.*, p. 768.

[16] Entry for May 31, 1920 in Crowley, *The Magical Record of the Beast 666*, ed. John Symonds and Kenneth Grant (Montréal: Next Step Publications and London: Duckworth, 1972), p. 137.

Every cause must produce its proper effect; so that, in this case, the son whom I willed to beget came to birth on a plane other than the material.... What I had really done was therefore to beget a Magical Son. So, precisely nine months afterwards, that is, at the summer solstice of 1916, Frater O.I.V. (the motto of C. Stansfeld Jones as a Probationer) entirely without my knowledge became a Babe of the Abyss.[17]

Crowley viewed this as a startling vindication of the A.'.A.'. system:

By means of my system of training, a man had crossed the Abyss and become a Master of the Temple in a much shorter period than had ever been known. My own case had been extraordinary. Eleven years had sufficed me to accomplish a task which in human experience had never required much less than triple the time.... In the case of O.I.V. the period was shorter still, and by much.... I could only conclude that his success was almost wholly due to the excellence of the system which I had given to the world. In short, it was the justification of my whole life, the unique and supreme reward of my immeasurable toils.[18]

Charles Robert Stansfeld Jones was born in London on April 2, 1886, and was an accountant by profession. Although his family was religious, he once remarked that "I was not at all addicted to religion in my youth."[19] He became interested in occultism when he was twenty; three years later, on December 24, 1909, he became a Probationer of A.'.A.'., taking the motto *Unus in Omnibus* ("one in all," abbreviated as V.I.O.). His instructor was Frater Per Ardua, Captain (later Major General) J. F. C. Fuller. Jones had only a few brief meetings with Crowley before moving to British Columbia in May of 1910, but maintained correspondence with A.'.A.'. headquarters in London. In 1913 he was passed to the grade of Neophyte, taking the motto Achad (the Hebrew for "one"). He was also an O.T.O. initiate, receiving the VII° *expedientiae causâ* around 1915 for his work in founding North America's first O.T.O. group, Agapae (later Agapé) Lodge. He would eventually become O.T.O. Grand Master X° for North America.

Liber Legis contains multiple references to a "child," and to "one" who would "follow" or "come after" the Beast with solutions to certain of its mysteries. Jones at first advanced no solutions; it was solely his miraculous attainment that prompted Crowley to recognize him as his "magical son." Crowley did not

[17] Crowley, *Confessions*, p. 801. [18] *Ibid.*, pp. 806-7.

[19] Charles Stansfeld Jones, letter to Albert Handel and Gerald Yorke, May 12, 1948.

initially consider a "magical son" to be synonymous with the "child" referred to in *Liber Legis*, but Jones lost no time in boldly claiming to be both. Crowley diplomatically replied: "I think the "child" means a real child. But of course you're the first-born of the Æon ... I belong in part to the old Æon, since I began under it."[20] But Crowley soon came to agree with Jones, and maintained this position for many years, naming Jones his heir in A∴A∴ and O.T.O. matters in the event of his death.

After his attainment of 1916 Jones assumed a new motto, V.I.O.O.I.V. (*Unus in Omnia, Omnia in Unum*). He took steps to pursue his magical work without interruption, leaving his job and, for a time, his wife Rubina. The following year he reversed his motto to O.I.V.V.I.O., and at the winter solstice had an illumination involving the word "AL," a Hebrew word for "God" or "existence." It was his first intimation of what would later be recognized as the Qabalistic key to *Liber Legis*.

In March of 1918 Jones sold all his possessions in order to come to New York and join Crowley, who was living on West 9th Street in Greenwich Village with Roddie Minor (Soror Ahitha), Hilarion's successor as Scarlet Woman. Crowley was writing *Liber Aleph* at this time; Jones evidently had arrived by the time chapter 168 was written. Crowley's longest recorded astral communication, the Amalantrah working, was in progress as well; the discarnate wizard Amalantrah gave Jones the name Arctæon. The working continued into the summer, when Crowley traveled up the Hudson River to camp on Esopus Island. Jones joined Crowley on his island retreat; whatever work the two magicians accomplished there can only be surmised, since Jones later destroyed the records.

By the fall of 1918 Crowley had moved to 1 University Place, on Washington Square. Here he and Jones formed ambitious plans to publish a new volume of *The Equinox* to promulgate the O.T.O. and A∴A∴ systems in America.

On October 7 and 8 Jones discovered that "AL," the "holy word" discovered the previous year, was the key to unlock certain of *Liber Legis*' mysteries. Curiously, he met with Crowley three days later and apparently made no mention of it. In November he set down his discoveries in a paper entitled *Liber 31*.[21] Again,

[20] Crowley, letter to Jones of July 1916; quoted in Jones, letter to Gerald Yorke, March 26, 1948.

he was strangely reticent; although he had originally intended to deliver *Liber 31* to Crowley immediately, he was to wait a full ten months before doing so.

By the following March Jones had moved to Detroit, where the first number of Volume Three of *The Equinox* had just been published. It included excerpts from Jones' diaries chronicling his magical career, just as Crowley's had been serialized in Volume One.[22] Jones was held up as an exemplar of the A∴A∴ system, as indeed he was. Crowley was sparing no effort to secure his son's future as a spiritual teacher.

The publication of Volume Three of *The Equinox* was to have been financed by the O.T.O. through the sale of its principal asset, Crowley's former residence Boleskine House on Loch Ness in Scotland, which he had donated to the O.T.O. in 1912. The sale failed to realize sufficient funds to complete the project, probably since Crowley's mortgage had been assumed by the Order at the time of the gift. Thus a subsequent number of *The Equinox*, to have been published in September of 1919, never appeared.

Jones chose this time to mail *Liber 31* to Crowley in New York. Crowley's response was ecstatic: "Your key opens Palace. [*Liber*] *CCXX* has opened like a flower. All solved, even II.76 & III.47."[23] Jones' keyword, "AL," adds to 31 by Hebrew gematria (א=1, ל=30; אל=31). This prompted Crowley to change the formal title of *The Book of the Law* from *Liber L vel Legis* to *Liber AL vel Legis*, and give the manuscript of *Liber Legis* the title *Liber XXXI* (not to be confused with Jones' work of the same number). Jones' Qabalistic proofs were intended for inclusion in an appendix to Crowley's commentaries to *Liber Legis*, but have been omitted in all editions published to date.

Crowley's reaction to Jones' discoveries can be shown by citing a few of the relevant verses of *Liber Legis* together with their commentaries:

> This book shall be translated into all tongues: but always with the original in the writing of the Beast; for in the chance shape of the letters and their position to one another: in these are mysteries that no Beast shall divine. Let him not seek to try: but one cometh after him,

---

[21] Charles Stanfield [*sic*] Jones, *Liber 31* (San Francisco: Level Press, 1974).

[22] The first installment of Jones' diaries appeared as "Liber CLXV, A Master of the Temple," *The Equinox* III(1), Detroit, 1919. Crowley's were serialized in abridged form as "Liber LVIII, The Temple of Solomon the King," *The Equinox* I(1-5, 8-10), London, 1909-13.

[23] Crowley, postcard to Jones of September 9, 1919; quoted in Jones, *Liber 31*.

whence I say not, who shall discover the Key of it all. Then this line drawn is a key; then this circle squared in its failure is a key also. And Abrahadabra. It shall be his child & that strangely. Let him not seek after this; for thereby alone can he fall from it. [*Liber Legis* III:47]

Crowley's brief commentary was "'one cometh after him': 'one', *i.e.* Achad. 'the Key of it all': all, *i.e.* AL 31 the Key."[24] He expands upon this in his *Confessions*:

The Book of the Law speaks of this "Child" as "One," as if with absolute vagueness. But the motto which Frater O.I.V. had taken on becoming a neophyte was "Achad" which is the Hebrew word for "One." It is further predicted that this "Child" shall discover the Key of the interpretation of the Book itself, and this I had been unable to do.... And in actual fact he did so discover that Key, two and a half years later.[25]

Crowley's comments to the following verses show his views both prior to, and following, Jones' discovery:

75. Aye! listen to the numbers & the words:
76. 4 6 3 8 A B K 2 4 A L G M O R 3 Y X 24 89 R P S T O V A L. What meaneth this, o prophet? Thou knowest not; nor shalt thou know ever. There cometh one to follow thee: he shall expound it. But remember, o chosen one, to be me; to follow the love of Nu in the star-lit heaven; to look forth upon men, to tell them this glad word. [*Liber Legis* II:75-76]

Crowley originally commented:

The passage ... appears to be a Qabalistic test (on the regular pattern) of any person who may claim to be the Magical Heir of The Beast. Be ye well assured all that the solution, when it is found, will be unquestionable. It will be marked by the most sublime simplicity, and carry immediate conviction.[26]

After Jones' discovery, he added:

The above paragraph was written previous to the communication of Charles Stansfeld Jones with regard to the "numbers and the words" which constitute the Key to the cipher of this Book. In the Appendix will be found the Qabalistic proofs referred to in the penultimate paragraph, as supporting the claim of Sir Charles Stansfeld Jones, whose occult names, numbers, dignities and titles, are as follows: PARZIVAL, Knight of the Holy Ghost, *etc.*, X° O.T.O., 418, 777, V.I.O. (*Unus in Omnibus*), Achad, or O.I.V.V.I.O. (*Omnia in Uno*, *Unus in Omnibus*), Fra.·. A.·.A.·., 8°=3□, Arctæon, to be my son by Jeanne Foster, Soror Hilarion.[26]

Jones wrote to Crowley on September 26, tentatively laying claim to the grade of Ipsissimus 10°=1□; he hints at this in *Liber*

[24] Crowley, New Comment to *Liber Legis* III:47.
[25] Crowley, *Confessions*, p. 801-2.
[26] Crowley, New Comment to *Liber Legis* II:75-76.

31. It was an early sign of his propensity to overreach himself, and a foreshadowing of future problems. Crowley traveled to Detroit that fall, and shortly after his return to New York, he set sail for Europe. It was the last he would see of the United States, or his magical son. The child was on his own.

After Crowley's departure, Jones lost no time in striking out in his own direction. He had apparently been chafing from an *Œdipus tyrannus* complex for some time. As early as 1916, Crowley had written *Liber CCC, Khabs Am Pekht*, "An Epistle of Therion 9°=2□ a Magus of A.'.A.'. to his Son,"[27] a precursor to *Liber Aleph*. Many years later, Jones remarked that

> Before the "child" had had much chance to do anything on its own account (or in accordance with its Will), 666 lost no time in formulating what he thought it should be expected to do — *viz*: his Will, more or less.[28]

Crowley's and Jones' difficulties began after Jones experienced a revelation that led him to rearrange the traditional paths of the Qabalistic Tree of Life. Crowley had presciently written Jones in 1916 that "it's true that as 8°=3□ one gets a sort of look round at the Supernal Triad, but it can only be a glimpse."[29] Jones' glimpse resulted in a series of books that disappointed Crowley.[30] He wrote:

> One who ought to have known better tried to improve the Tree of Life by turning the Serpent of Wisdom upside down! Yet he could not even make his scheme symmetrical: his little remaining good sense revolted at the supreme atrocities. Yet he succeeded in reducing the whole Magical Alphabet to nonsense, and shewing that he had never understood its real meaning.[31]

This was written for publication; Crowley's deeper concern was for Jones himself, as is apparent from his diary:

> The point is this — the books — even apart from the absurd new attributions proposed for the Paths — are so hopelessly bad in almost every way — English, style, sense, point of view, oh everything! — yet they may do good to the people they are written for. My real concern is lest [Jones] get too much *ubris* & come a real cropper.[32]

---

[27] Published in *The Equinox* III(1), Detroit, 1919; see also *The Equinox* III(10) (New York, 1986: reprinted York Beach, ME: Weiser, 1990).

[28] Jones, letter to Gerald Yorke, March 26, 1948.

[29] *Ibid.*

[30] Frater Achad [Charles Stansfeld Jones], *Q.B.L., or The Bride's Reception* (1922), *The Egyptian Revival* (1923) and *The Anatomy of the Body of God* (1925), privately printed, Chicago; reprinted in 1969 by Samuel Weiser, New York.

[31] Crowley, *Magick in Theory and Practice*, p. 7n.

[32] Crowley, entry for August 9, 1923, in *The Magical Diaries of Aleister Crowley*, ed. Stephen Skinner (Jersey: Neville Spearman and New York: Samuel Weiser, 1979), p. 127.

In 1921, Jones was appointed North American Grand Master X° of O.T.O. by Theodor Reuss, who as Frater Superior and Outer Head of the Order (O.H.O.) was its international head. Crowley had been British Grand Master since 1912 (as Baphomet X°). Reuss died in 1923, and according to Crowley, "in the O.H.O.'s last letter to me he invited me to become his successor as O.H.O. and Frater Superior."[33] Crowley's first act as O.H.O. was to reconfirm the charters of Jones (Parzival X°) as Grand Master for North America and Heinrich Tränker (Recnartus X°) as Grand Master for Germany; they reciprocated by confirming Crowley in office. But however fraternal their formal dealings, Crowley remained highly critical of Jones' Qabalistic theories. By 1924, Crowley was in North Africa, and he wrote to Jones in Chicago:

> You seem to have no means of judging the limits of your scholarship and it's of supreme importance that you write nothing which initiated scholars can criticize adversely.... It is quite possible to be too great a Qabalist. You must buttress your work by that of other thinkers, even if profane.[34]

In addition to leading the German O.T.O., Heinrich Tränker operated the *Collegium Pansophicum*; Jones was its representative in North America. It was among the first of many esoteric orders with which Jones would become involved; another such order provided the funds for Jones' livelihood.

In 1925 Crowley traveled to Weida, in Thuringia, Germany, for a conference of leading German esoteric groups. During his visit he met Karl Germer, who edited the journal *Pansophia*. On learning that Jones' books had been translated for publication, Crowley took matters into his own hands and corrected Jones' unorthodox Qabalistic attributions. Addressing Jones as "my beloved Son," Crowley wrote to explain his actions:

> You must be completely insane with megalomania — as you have been warned often enough that this was your greatest danger — to take friendly criticism like this as "an impertinence." There are no opinions on the other side among serious people: it is unanimously held that your books, while they contain much excellent work in the popular presentation of the ideas learnt from The Equinox and the Order, are calculated to arouse ridicule by their crudeness, lack of originality, and egoism. The style of "sublime" passages is sheer imitation of mine. There are some lapses which are utterly incomprehensible to me. Notably certain equations are given as Qabalistic

33 Crowley, letter to Jones, dated ☉ in ♑, Anno XX (Dec. 1924 - Jan. 1925.)
34 *Ibid.*

"*proof*" which are nothing of the sort. You, of all people, whom I took to know better than any one else alive what Qabalistic proof really means!... Incidentally, how a supposed $8^\circ = 3^\square$ can talk about "Infallible Reason," baffles that very fallible quality in me!... I can only repeat once again my very serious warning that unless you kill out that inflamed ego, go back and steadily work through the grades you jumped so gaily, and adopt an attitude of probity and brotherhood with your fellow-workers, you will come to the most almighty everlasting smash in the history of — Chicago!... P.S.: I blame myself most severely for having tacitly acquiesced in your giving up your work as an accountant. It is an absolute breach of the regulations of A.'.A.'. to accept money — under whatever disguise — in return for "occult" teaching.[35]

Crowley's ambivalance shows in his closing: "ever your anxious and affectionate sire."

It was not long before the first break in their relationship occurred; ironically, its cause was not at all magical, but entirely mundane. When he left the United States for Europe, Crowley had left a valuable book collection in Jones' safekeeping, who placed it with a Detroit storage warehouse. Crowley later asked Jones to produce the books, but one of two boxes containing the most valuable items could not be found; it had been lost by the storage firm. While Crowley was convinced that Jones had stolen it, Jones maintained his innocence, his honor deeply offended by Crowley's suggestion. Jones was in fact innocent, as the books were found by the warehouse after both men were long dead.[36] But the incident effectively ended communication for many years.

New problems of a more magical character began to develop, which were to multiply over the ensuing years. These would eventually lead Crowley to conclude that Jones was a failure, but he reached this view gradually and with great reluctance.

Two years later, in 1928, Jones returned to England, probably to visit his family. The next development is surprising; he recounts what transpired, writing of himself (as Achad) in the third person:

It was necessary for Achad to be led to the opposite Pillar of the Temple there to learn the mysteries of the R[oman] C[atholic] Church. He became an orthodox member of that Church and received his first communion at Midnight Mass, Christmas, 1928. This step, and this

35 Crowley, letter to Jones, dated , dated ☉ in ♋, ☾ in ♉, Anno XXI (July-August 1925).

36 These books now form an important part of the major collection of Crowleyana at the Harry Ransom Humanities Research Center at the University of Texas in Austin.

alone, led to the opening of the Initiations and Ordeals which were to follow in accordance with *Liber Legis*.[37]

Jones took confirmation in Roman Catholicism in 1929, taking the name John. He wrote many years later that "I discovered that the combined names had a certain Qabalistic significance: Charles Robert Iohn Stansfeld Iones [*i.e.* CHRISTI].)"[38] (Amusingly, the American magician C. F. Russell, who at times detested Jones, had "christened" him "Jesus Stansfeld Christ" nearly ten years earlier.)

Jones' mention of "the Initiations and Ordeals which were to follow in accordance with *Liber Legis*" refers to the following verses in Chapter III:

> 63. The fool readeth this Book of the Law, and its comment; & he understandeth it not.
> 64. Let him come through the first ordeal, & it will be to him as silver.
> 65. Through the second, gold.
> 66. Through the third, stones of precious water.
> 67. Through the fourth, ultimate sparks of the intimate fire.

Many years later Jones would summarize his experience of these ordeals:

> The first ordeal had been successfully passed in 1932 and was marked by "The Arising of the Silver Star." The second ordeal was passed and marked by the arising of the Golden Star the following year. The third ordeal and formulation of the Nine-fold Diamond occurred in 1935. The fourth ordeal "ultimate sparks of the intimate fire" was of 1945. It began on July 16th (without any knowledge of events at [Los] Alamos) and was over two days *before* the first announcement of the dropping of an Atomic bomb on Hiroshima.[39]

Jones communicated the news of his 1932 Silver Star Ordeal not only to Crowley, but to the Catholic Church as well. He developed a conviction that the Æon of Horus was ending, and a new Æon of Truth and Justice — ruled by the Egyptian goddess Maat (or Ma) — was imminent.

In 1936 Crowley resumed their fitful correspondence. In his preparations for the publication of *The Equinox of the Gods*, Crowley included Jones in the A.'.A.'. *imprimatur* under three of Jones' mottos: Achad, Parsival and 777. He wrote to Jones that July, politely criticizing his latest revelations and encouraging him to make a fresh start:

---

37 Jones, letter to Gerald Yorke and Albert Handel, May 5, 1948.

38 *Ibid.*, May 12, 1948.

39 *Ibid.*, May 5, 1948.

Your preparations for the Æon of Justice seem to me personal to yourself, incidents in the course of your initiation and I have no doubt that they will flower at the fall of the Great Equinox. But I think that your position in respect to the Æon of Horus is to be considered of supreme importance at this juncture. I do not think your work in respect of *The Book of the Law* has passed beyond its beginning. I regard the curious experiences through which you have passed as the necessary training for your full assumption of office.[40]

Jones interpreted this as "proof" that Crowley "recognized the possibility of [the] Æon of Truth and Justice coming in."[41] But proof was scarcely necessary; it was not Jones but Crowley himself who had first expounded the future Æon of Ma, in his commentaries to *Liber Legis*. He taught that Justice was a complimentary ideal to the realities of the present Æon, and a goal toward which mankind should strive. Citing the close interrelationship in the Tarot between Leo (Atu XI, *Strength*) and Libra (Atu VIII, *Justice* or *Adjustment*), he wrote that between Horus and Maat

There is no such violent antithesis as that between Osiris and Horus; Strength will prepare the Reign of Justice. We should begin already, as I deem, to regard this Justice as the Ideal whose way we should make ready, by virtue of our Force and Fire.[42]

It is evident, however, that Crowley did not share Jones' belief that a "Great Equinox" heralding the Æon of Truth and Justice was imminent. But before they could have a full exchange of views, their relationship ended abruptly. In 1936, just as *The Equinox of the Gods* was being published, Jones wrote a pseudonymous attack on *Liber Legis* which he tried to have published in the London journal *The Occult Review*. He also invoked his authority as O.T.O. Grand Master X° for North America to attempt the closure of Agapé Lodge in California, founded by former Vancouver lodge member Wilfred Talbot Smith. These problems, together with Crowley's mistaken belief that Jones had stolen from him, led Crowley to take a drastic step. Notwithstanding Jones' high rank of X° *ad vitam*, he was summarily expelled from the O.T.O. The expulsion notice was to be his last direct communication from Crowley, and even this was sent indirectly, forwarded by W. T. Smith. Jones' later attempts to make contact through third parties caused Crowley to comment dismissively:

---

40 Crowley, July 22, 1936, quoted in Jones, letter to Gerald Yorke, April 1, 1948.
41 Jones, letter to Gerald Yorke, April 1, 1948.
42 Crowley, New Comment to *Liber Legis* III:34.

With regard to Achad's communications: I can make no sense of any of them, and shall ignore the whole matter. Achad went completely insane in the strict medico-legal sense of the term in 1925, and he has been getting deeper in ever since.[43]

Crowley always honored Jones as the discoverer of the key to *Liber Legis*. But as early as 1920 he had speculated that there might be more than one "child," and he eventually came to consider the "child" as distinct from the "one" referred to in *The Book of the Law*.[44] In an undated postscript to his commentary to *Liber Legis*, Crowley outlined what may well have been his final position, acknowledging the possibility that Jones may have become a Black Brother:

This "one" is not to be confused with the "child" referred to elsewhere in this book. It is quite possible that O.I.V.V.I.O. (who took the grade 8°=3▫ by an act of will without going through the lower grades in the regular way) failed to secure complete annihilation in crossing the Abyss; so that the drops of blood which should have been cast in the Cup of Babalon should "breed scorpions, and vipers, and the Cat of Slime." In this case he would develop into a Black Brother, to be torn in pieces and reduced to his Elements against his will.[45]

This doctrine is embodied in *The Vision and the Voice*, a work Jones knew well, and cited frequently; it was part of his Probationer reading curriculum in the A.'.A.'..[46] But Jones had taken the Oath of the Abyss before A.'.A.'. doctrine was fully and formally codified.[47] Taking a strict interpretation of the Oath, he would later assert, with some justification, that

All this business about "draining every drop into the Cup of Babalon" *etc.* is entirely a matter of A.C.'s own invention so far as any Oath of M[agister] T[empli] is concerned. The Oath of an M. T. of A.'.A.'. is to interpret every event as a direct dealing of God with the soul. This I have tried to do, that is all I set out to do when entering the Abyss in 1916. This is all A.C. ever said should be done.[48]

Crowley died in Hastings, England on December 1, 1947, leaving the reins of the O.T.O. and A.'.A.'. in the hands of Karl Germer in New York. News of Crowley's death triggered a torrent of communications from Jones to his trusted student

43 Crowley, letter to Karl Germer, July 3, 1946.

44 Crowley, *The Equinox of the Gods*, p. 127n, and New Comment to *Liber Legis* II:76.

45 Crowley, New Comment to *Liber Legis* II:76.

46 [Crowley], "The Vision and the Voice," 10th and 11th Æthyrs.

47 For the Oath of the Abyss, see *The Equinox* III(10), p. 18. Many facets of the A.'.A.'. system were first codified formally in "One Star in Sight," *Magick in Theory and Practice* (1929-30), Appendix II.

48 Jones, postscript to letter to Gerald Yorke, April 1, 1948.

Albert Handel in New York, and to the archivist Gerald Yorke in London; copies of certain of these were sent to Karl Germer as well. Jones candidly speaks his mind in these letters, releasing the pent-up frustration of three decades. In the magical rebellion of a magical child, he declared that the Æon of Truth and Justice had commenced on April 2, 1948 at 1.11 P.M. He was at pains to stress that this Æon "is *not* precisely the same as the Æon of Ma (or MA-ION) which was first mentioned, as such, in a document written April 14, at 1.06 P.M."[49] He refrained from claiming the grade of Magus 9°=2□, but even his demurral is disturbing if it is borne in mind that in thelemic Qabalah, the "false sephira" Daäth is the lonely outpost of the Black Brothers:

> I have never claimed to be a Magus. (I might temporarily have become one in 1920 when I proclaimed that word "Love" which we now suggest using for current Equinox. If so, it was an "accident" or "chance" so to speak.) If this New Æon is what it seems to be, it will have lifted the Curse of Magus and destroyed the Glamour and Lies and Madness of the Supernal Paths. That would leave one in Daäth — and represent real Attainment — the becoming one with Those Who Know.[50]

Jones did not challenge Crowley's Will, but expressed grave doubts concerning Germer's fitness to succeed Crowley. While he overcame his reservations over Germer's lack of formal magical training, it would only have been human to feel some resentment at having been disinherited. But it is clear from his letters that his revelations after Crowley's death were not conceived in a vacuum. They not only helped him cut his ties to his magical father; he claimed that they superceded Crowley's life's work:

> After A.C. is dead, and the Will in favour of Saturnus [Germer], imagine what [Germer] feels when ... Achad crops up and in no way opposes the Will, but produces a New Æon, which throws the whole magical formula of A.C. and Saturnus out of gear and into the discard as out of date.[51]

Charles Stansfeld Jones died in British Columbia in 1950, leaving a doubtful spiritual legacy. He remains an exemplary student of the A.·.A.·. system of attainment, as an objective reading of his diaries will show. But as Karl Germer observed, Jones developed in the "pre-Comment" period; that is, before the writing of the 1925 "Short Comment" to *Liber Legis* that

---

49 Jones, letter to Gerald Yorke and Albert Handel, May 16, 1948.

50 Jones, letter to Gerald Yorke, April 17, 1948.

51 Jones, letter to Gerald Yorke and Albert Handel, May 24, 1948.

forbade commentary on the book.[51] Such commentary led Jones to glory; some would assert that it also led to his downfall. His published works have reached only a small audience; some of these are unjustly neglected. But Jones is celebrated to this day as the discoverer of the Qabalistic key to *Liber Legis*, and for his pioneering work on behalf of the North American O.T.O. In retrospect, his is one of the cautionary tales of the Path of the Wise.

Liber Aleph was originally scheduled to appear as *The Equinox* III(4) around 1939, and was again in press at Crowley's death in 1947. He never saw the proofs; the funds for its publication were found under his deathbed. Its first edition was posthumously issued in 1962 as *The Equinox* III(6), edited by Karl Germer and Marcelo Motta. It was the last of the major Crowley works edited and published by Germer, as he died the following year.

This second edition of *Liber Aleph* relies on three principal sources: the holograph manuscript in the Yorke Collection in London, a typescript from the Germer Accession of the O.T.O. Archives, and the 1962 first edition. Over the years, Crowley made several significant changes to the work, all of which have been retained. But many "scribal glosses" and textual elisions occur in both the typescript and the first edition; these have been corrected by reference to the original manuscript. While only minor corrections have been made to the Latin chapter titles, their English translations required significant changes. For the benefit of those readers who (like the present editor) lack Latin, these English translations are supplied on each page. The Greek chapter numbers appeared in both manuscript and typescript, but not the first edition; these have been restored. The index to the first edition has been replaced, and is here subdivided into three sections. The first section consists of general entries; the second lists specific technical terms pertaining to Qabalah, Tarot and astrology. The last section indexes the many direct quotations from *Liber Legis* by chapter and verse, since *Liber Aleph* was considered by Crowley to constitute a commentary to *Liber Legis*.

---

[51] For the "Short Comment" see *The Holy Books of Thelema* (*The Equinox* III(9); York Beach, ME: Weiser, 1983, reprinted 1989), p. 196.

Aleister Crowley needs no apologist, but it is important to bear in mind that *Liber Aleph* is addressed to one individual at a particular stage of spiritual development. Certain chapters of *Liber Aleph* are often taken out of this context, and hence misunderstood. One such passage may be found in chapter 133, where Crowley adjures his son to "tell not the Truth to any Woman." As Virginia Woolf once pointed out, Samuel Butler had it that a wise man should not speak the truth *about* woman. Whether Crowley's words on this subject are wisdom or folly, they do deserve to be read in their original context. This is not to say that *Liber Aleph* does not contain much spiritual counsel of wide application.

I wish to thank William E. Heidrick, Frater A. and Frater Φ. for their production, proofreading and research assistance, and John P. Otte and Jeannine Bradley for invaluable editorial advice. I am grateful to the curators of the Yorke Collection in London for providing access to the original manuscript of *Liber Aleph*, and to the O.T.O. Archives for access to the unpublished correspondence of Aleister Crowley, Charles Stansfeld Jones and others. I would especially like to thank Martin P. Starr for his generous assistance; without his expertise, many longstanding textual problems would have remained uncorrected. Any editorial follies are entirely my own.

Love is the law, love under will.

Hymenaeus Beta X°
Frater Superior, O. T. O.

Agapé Grand Lodge
New York City
Spring Equinox, Anno IIIxxi
March 20, 1991 EV

LIBER
ALEPH
VEL CXI
THE BOOK OF
WISDOM OR
FOLLY
IN THE FORM OF
AN EPISTLE OF
666
THE GREAT
WILD BEAST
TO HIS SON
777

A∴A∴ Publication in Class B.

α

APOLOGIA

HAVE BEGOTTEN THEE, O MY SON, AND that strangely, as thou knowest, upon the Scarlet Woman called Hilarion, as it was mysteriously foretold unto me in *The Book of the Law*. Now therefore that thou art come to the Age of Understanding, do thou give ear unto my Wisdom, for that therein lieth a simple and direct Way for every Man that he may attain to the End.

Firstly, then, I would have thee to know that Spiritual Experience and Perfection have no necessary Connexion with Advancement in Our Holy Order. But for each Man is a Path: there is a Constant, and there is a Variable. Seek ever therefore in thy Work of the Promulgation of the Law to discover in each Man his own true Nature.

For in each Man his Inmost Light is the Core of his Star. That is, Hadit; and his Work is the Identification of himself with that Light.

It is not every Man who is called to the sublime Task of the A.·.A.·., wherein he must master thoroughly every Detail of the Great Work, so that he may in due Season accomplish it not only for himself, but for all who are bound unto him. There are very many for whom in their present Incarnations this Great Work may be impossible; since their appointed Work may be in Satisfaction of some Magical Debt, or in Adjustment of some Balance, or in Fulfilment of some Defect. As is written: *Suum Cuique*.

Now because thou art the Child of my Bowels, I yearn greatly towards thee, o my Son, and I strive strongly with my Spirit that by my Wisdom I may make plain thy Way before thee; and thus in many Chapters will I write for thee those Things that may profit thee. *Sis benedictus*.

β

DE ARTE KABBALISTICA

O THOU STUDY MOST CONSTANTLY, MY SON, in the Art of the Holy Qabalah. Know that herein the Relations between Numbers, though they be mighty in Power and prodigal of Knowledge, are but lesser Things. For the Work is to reduce all other Conceptions to these of Number, because thus thou wilt lay bare the very Structure of thy Mind, whose rule is Necessity rather than Prejudice. Not until the Universe is thus laid naked before thee canst thou truly anatomize it. The Tendencies of thy Mind lie deeper far than any Thought, for they are the Conditions and the Laws of Thought; and it is these that thou must bring to Naught.

This Way is most sure; most sacred; and the Enemies thereof most awful, most sublime. It is for the Great Souls to enter on this Rigour and Austerity. To Them the Gods themselves do Homage; for it is the Way of Utmost Purity.

γ

DE VITA CORRIGENDA

NOW, SON, THAT THE TRUE PRINCIPLE of Self-control is Liberty. For we are born into a World which is in Bondage to Ideals; to them we are perforce fitted, even as his Enemies to the Bed of Procrustes. Each of us, as he groweth, learns Repression of himself and his True Will. "It is a lie, this folly against self": these Words are written in *The Book of the Law*. So therefore those Passions in ourselves which we understand to be Hindrances are nor Art nor Part of our True Will, but diseased Appetites, manifest in us through false early Training. Thus the Tabus of savage Tribes in such a matter as Love constrain that True Love which is born in us; and by this Constraint come ills of Body and Mind. Either the Force of Repression carries it, and creates Neuroses and Insanities; or the Revolt against that Force, breaking forth with Violence, involves Excesses and Extravagances. All these Things are Disorders, and against Nature. Now then learn of me the Testimony of History and Literature, as a great Scroll of Learning. But the Vellum of the Scroll is of Man's Skin, and its Ink of his Heart's Blood.

δ

LEGENDA DE AMORE

THE FAULT, THAT IS FATALITY, IN LOVE, as in every other Form of Will, is Impurity. It is not the Spontaneity thereof which worketh Woe, but some Repression in the Environment.

In the Fable of Adam and Eve is this great Lesson taught by the Masters of the Holy Qabalah. For Love were to them the eternal Eden, save for the Repression signified by the Tree of the Knowledge of Good and Evil. Thus their Nature of Love was perfect; it was their Fall from that Innocence which drove them from the Garden.

In the Love of Romeo and Juliet was no Flaw; but family Feud, which imported nothing to that Love, was its Bane; and the Rashness and Violence of their Revolt against that Repression, slew them.

In the pure Outrush of natural Love in Desdemona for Othello was no Flaw; but his Love was marred by his Consciousness of his Age and his Race, of the Prejudices of his Fellows and of his own Experience of Woman-frailty.

E

GESTA DE AMORE

OW AS LITERATURE OVERFLOWETH WITH THE Murders of Love, so also doth History, and the Lesson is ever the same.

Thus the Loves of Abelard and of Heloise were destroyed by the System of Repression in which they chanced to move.

Thus Beatrice was robbed of Dante by social Artificialities and Paolo slain on account of Things external to his Love of Francesca.

Then, *per contra*, Martin Luther, being a Giant of Will, and also the Eighth Henry of England, as a mighty King, bent them to overturn the whole World that they might have satisfaction of their Loves.

And who shall follow them? For even now we find great Churchmen, Statesmen, Princes, Dramamakers, and many lesser Men, overwhelmed utterly and ruined by the Conflict between their Passions and the Society about them. Wherein which Party errs is no matter of Moment for our Thought; but the Existence of that War is Evidence of Wrong done to Nature.

F

ULTIMA THESIS DE AMORE

THEREFORE, O MY SON, BE THOU WARY, NOT bowing before the false Idols and Ideals, yet not flaming forth in Fury against them, unless that be thy Will.

But in this Matter be prudent and be silent, discerning subtly and with Acumen the Nature of the Will within thee; so that thou mistake not Fear for Chastity, or Anger for Courage. And since the Fetters are old and heavy, and thy Limbs withered and distorted by reason of their Compulsion, do thou, having broken them, walk gently for a little while, until the ancient Elasticity return, so that thou mayst walk, run, and leap naturally and with Rejoicing.

Also, since these Fetters are as a Bond almost universal, be instant to declare the Law of Liberty, and the full Knowledge of all Truth that appertaineth to this Matter; for if in this only thou overcome, then shall all Earth be free, taking its Pleasure in Sunlight without Fear or Phrenzy. Amen.

ζ

DE NATURA SUA PERCIPIENDA

NDERSTAND, O MY SON, IN THY YOUTH, these Words which some wise One, now nameless, spake of old: except ye become as little Children, ye shall in no wise enter into the Kingdom of Heaven. This is to say that thou must first comprehend thine original Nature in every Point, as it was before thou wast forced to bow before the Gods of Wood and Stone that Men have made, not comprehending the Law of Change, and of Evolution Through Variation, and the independent Value of every Living Soul.

Learn this also, that even the Will to the Great Work may be misunderstood of Men; for this Work must proceed naturally and without Overstress, as all true Works. Right also is that Word that the Kingdom of Heaven suffereth Violence, and the violent take it by Force. But except thou be violent by Virtue of thy true Nature, how shalt thou take it? Be not as the Ass in the Lion's Skin; but if thou be born Ass, bear patiently thy Burdens, and enjoy thy Thistles; for an Ass also, as in the Fables of Apuleius and of Matthias, may come to Glory in the Path of his own Virtue.

On Comprehending one's Nature

η

ALTERA DE VIA NATURAE

SAYEST THOU (METHINKS) THAT HERE IS A great Riddle, since by Reason of much Repression thou hast lost the Knowledge of thine original Nature?

My Son, this is not so; for by a peculiar Ordinance of Heaven, and a Disposition occult within his Mind, is every Man protected from this Loss of his own Soul, until and unless he be by Choronzon disintegrated and dispersed beyond power of Will to repair, as when the Conflict within him, rending and burning, hath made his Mind utterly Desert, and his Soul Madness.

Give Ear, give Ear attentively; the Will is not lost; though it be buried beneath a life-old midden of Repressions, for it persisteth vital within thee (is it not the true Motion of thine inmost Being?) and for all thy conscious Striving, cometh forth by Night and by Stealth in Dream and Phantasy. Now is it naked and brilliant, now clothed in rich Robes of Symbol and Hieroglyph; but alway travelleth it with thee upon thy Path, ready to acquaint thee with thy true Nature, if thou attend unto its Word, its Gesture, or its Show of Imagery.

θ

QUO MODO NATURA SUA EST LEGENDA

EEM NOT THEREFORE THAT THY LIGHTEST Fancy is witless: it is a Word to thee, a Prophecy, a Sign or Signal from thy Lord. Thy most unconscious Acts are Keys to the Treasure-Chamber of thine own Palace, which is the House of the Holy Ghost. Consider well thy conscious Thoughts and Acts, for they are under the Dominion of thy Will, and moved in Accord with the Operation of thy Reason; this indeed is a necessary Work, enabling thee to comprehend in what manner thou mayst adjust thyself to thine Environment. Yet is this Adaptation but Defence for the most Part, or at the best Subterfuge and Stratagem in the Tactics of thy Life, with but an accidental and subordinate Relation to thy True Will, whereof by Consciousness and by Reason thou mayst be ignorant, unless by Fortune great and rare thou be already harmonized in thyself, the Outer with the Inner, which Grace is not common among Men, and is the Reward of previous Attainment.

Neglect not simple Introspection, therefore, but give yet greater Heed unto those Dreams and Phantasies, those Gestures and Manners unconscious, and of undiscovered Cause, which betoken thee.

On how one's own Nature should be Examined

DE SOMNIIS

a. CAUSA PER ACCIDENS

As all Diseases have two conjunct Causes, one immediate, external and exciting, the other constitutional, internal, and predisposing, so it is with Dreams, which are Dis-eases, or unbalanced States, of Consciousness, Disturbers of Sleep as Thoughts are of Life.

This exciting Cause is commonly of two kinds: *videlicet*, *imprimis*, the physical Condition of the Sleeper, as a Dream of Water caused by a Shower without, or a Dream of Strangulation caused by a Dyspnœa, or a Dream of Lust caused by the seminal Congestions of an unclean Life, or a Dream of falling or flying caused by some unstable Equilibrium of his Body.

Secundo, the psychical Condition of the Sleeper, the Dream being determined by recent Events in his Life, usually those of the Day previous, and especially such Events as have caused Excitement or Anxiety, the more so if they be unfinished or unfulfilled.

But this exciting Cause is of a superficial Nature, as it were a Cloke or a Mask; and thus it but lendeth Aspect to the other Cause, which lieth in the Nature of the Sleeper himself.

 ❦ *On Dreams.*
(a) External Causes

DE SOMNIIS

β. CAUSA PER NATURAM

HE DEEP, CONSTITUTIONAL, OR PREDISposing Cause of Dreams lieth within the Jurisdiction of the Will itself. For that Will, being alway present, albeit (it may be) latent, discovereth himself when no longer inhibited by that conscious Control which is determined by Environment, and therefore oft times contrary to himself. This being so, the Will declareth himself, as it were in a Pageant, and sheweth himself thus apparelled, unto the Sleeper, for a Warning or Admonition. Every Dream, or Pageant of Fancy, is therefore a Shew of Will; and Will being no more prevented by Environment or by Consciousness, cometh as a Conqueror. Yet even so he must come for the most Part throned upon the Chariot of the Exciting Cause of the Dream, and therefore is his Appearance symbolic, like a Writing in Cipher, or like a Fable, or like a Riddle in Pictures. But alway doth he triumph and fulfil himself therein, for the Dream is a natural Compensation in the inner World for any Failure of Achievement in the outer.

On Dreams.
(b) Innate Causes

λ

De Somniis

γ. Vestimenta Horroris

Now then if in a Dream the Will be alway triumphant, how cometh it that a Man may be ridden of the Nightmare? And of this the true Explanation is that in such a case the Will is in Danger, having been attacked and wounded, or corrupted by the Violence of some Repression. Thus the Consciousness of the Will is directed to the sore Spot, as in Pain, and seeketh Comfort in an Externalization, or Shew, of that Antagonism. And because the Will is sacred, such Dreams excite an Ecstasy or Phrenzy of Horror, Fear, or Disgust. Thus the True Will of Œdipus was toward the Bed of Jocasta, but the Tabu, strong both by Inheritance and by Environment, was so attached to that Will that his Dream concerning his Destiny was a Dream of Fear and of Abhorrence, his Fulfilment thereof (even in Ignorance) a Spell to stir up all the subconscious Forces of all the People about him, and his Realization of the Act a Madness potent to drive him to self-inflicted Blindness and fury-haunted Exile.

 On Dreams.
(c) Clothed with Horror

μ

DE SOMNIIS

δ. SEQUENTIA

KNOW FIRMLY, O MY SON, THAT THE TRUE Will cannot err; for it is thine appointed Course in Heaven, in whose Order is Perfection.

A Dream of Horror is therefore the most serious of all Warnings; for it signifieth that thy Will, which is Thy Self in respect of its Motion, is in Affliction and Danger. Thus thou must instantly seek out the Cause of that subconscious Conflict, and destroy thine Enemy utterly by bringing thy conscious Vigour as an Ally to that True Will. If then there be a Traitor in that Consciousness, how much the more is it necessary for thee to arise and extirpate him before he wholly infect thee with the divided Purpose which is the first Breach in that Fortress of the Soul whose Fall should bring it to the shapeless Ruin whose Name is Choronzon!

On Dreams.
(d) Continuation

V

DE SOMNIIS

ε. CLAVICULA

HE DREAM DELIGHTFUL IS THEN A Pageant of the Fulfilment of the True Will, and the Nightmare a symbolic Battle between it and its Assailants in thyself. But there can be only one True Will, even as there can be only one proper Motion in any Body, no Matter of how many Forces that Motion be the Resultant. Seek therefore this Will, and conjoin with it thy conscious Self; for this is that which is written: "thou hast no right but to do thy will. Do that, and no other shall say nay." Thou seest, o my Son, that all conscious Opposition to thy Will, whether in Ignorance, or by Obstinacy, or through Fear of others, may in the End endanger even thy True Self, and bring thy Star into Disaster.

And this is the true Key to Dreams; see that thou be diligent in its Use, and unlock therewith the secret Chambers of thine Heart.

ξ

De Via per Empyraeum

ONCERNING THY TRAVELLINGS IN THE Body of Light, or Astral Journeys and Visions so-called, do thou lay this Wisdom to thine Heart, o my Son, that in this Practice, whether Things Seen and Heard be Truth and Reality, or whether they be Phantoms in the Mind, abideth this supreme Magical Value, namely: Whereas the Direction of such Journeys is consciously willed, and determined by Reason, and also unconsciously willed, by the True Self, since without It no Invocation were possible, we have here a Cooperation or Alliance between the Inner and the Outer Self, and thus an Accomplishment, at least partial, of the Great Work.

And therefore is Confusion or Terror in any such Practice an Error fearful indeed, bringing about Obsession, which is a temporary or even it may be a permanent Division of the Personality, or Insanity, and therefore a Defeat most fatal and pernicious, a Surrender of the Soul to Choronzon.

On Travel through the Empyrean

0

De Cultu

Now, O my Son, that thou mayst be well guarded against thy ghostly Enemies, do thou work constantly by the Means prescribed in our Holy Books.

Neglect never the fourfold Adorations of the Sun in his four Stations, for thereby thou dost affirm thy Place in Nature and her Harmonies.

Neglect not the Performance of the Ritual of the Pentagram, and of the Assumption of the Form of Hoor-pa-Kraat.

Neglect not the daily Miracle of the Mass, either by the Rite of the Gnostic Catholic Church, or that of the Phœnix.

Neglect not the Performance of the Mass of the Holy Ghost, as Nature Herself prompteth thee.

Travel much also in the Empyrean in thy Body of Light, seeking ever Abodes more fiery and lucid.

Finally, exercise constantly the Eight Limbs of Yoga. And so shalt thou come to the End.

π

De Clavicula Somniorum

ND NOW CONCERNING MEDITATION LET ME disclose unto thee more fully the Mystery of the Key of Dreams and Phantasies.

Learn first that as the Thought of the Mind standeth before the Soul and hindereth its Manifestation in Consciousness, so also the gross physical Will is the Creator of the Dreams of common Men. And as in Meditation thou dost destroy every Thought by mating it with its Opposite, so must thou cleanse thyself by a full and perfect Satisfaction of that bodily Will in the Way of Chastity and Holiness which hath been revealed unto thee in thine Initiation.

This inner Silence of the Body being attained, it may be that the True Will may speak in True Dreams; for it is written that He giveth unto His Beloved in Sleep.

Prepare thyself therefore in this Way, as a good Knight should do.

♀

DE SOMNO LUCIDO

NOW KNOW THIS ALSO, THAT AT THE END of that secret Way lieth a Garden wherein is a Rest House prepared for thee.

For to him whose physical Needs (of whatsoever kind) are not truly satisfied cometh a physical or lunar Sleep appointed to refresh and recreate by Cleansing and Repose; but on him that is bodily pure the Lord bestoweth a solar or lucid Sleep, wherein move Images of pure Light fashioned by the True Will. And this is called by the Qabalists the Sleep of Shiloam, and of this doth also Porphyry make mention, and Cicero, with many other Wise Men of Old Time.

Compare, o my Son, with this Doctrine that which was taught thee in the Sanctuary of the Gnosis concerning the Death of the Righteous; and learn moreover that these are but particular Cases of an Universal Formula.

ρ

DE VENENIS

Y SON, IF THOU FAST AWHILE, THERE shall come unto thee a second State of physiological Being, in which is a Delight passive and equable, without Will, a Contentment of Weakness, with a Feeling of Lightness and of Purity. And this is because the Blood hath absorbed, in its Need of Nutriment, all foreign Elements. Such also is the Case with the Mind which hath not fed itself on Thought. Consider the placid and ruminant Existence of such Persons as read little, are removed from worldly Struggle by some sufficient Property of small and unexciting Value, stably invested, and by Age and Environment are free from Passion. They live, according to their own Nature, without Desire, and they oppose no Resistance to the Operations of Time. Such are called happy, and in their Way of Vegetable Life it is so; for they are free of any Poison.

σ

DE MOTU VITAE

EARN THEN, O MY SON, THAT ALL PHEnomena are the Effect of Conflict, even as the Universe itself is a Nothing expressed as the Difference of two Equalities, or, an thou wilt, as the Divorce of Nuit and Hadit. So therefore every Marriage dissolveth a more material, and createth a less material Complex; and this is our Way of Love, rising ever from Ecstasy to Ecstasy. So then all high Violence, that is to say, all Consciousness, is the spiritual Orgasm of a Passion between two lower and grosser Opposites. Thus Light and Heat result from the Marriage of Hydrogen and Oxygen, Love from that of Man and Woman, Dhyana or Ecstasy from that of the Ego and the non-Ego.

But be thou well grounded in this Thesis corollary, that one or two such Marriages do but destroy for a Time the Exacerbation of any Complex; to deracinate such is a Work of long Habit and deep Search in Darkness for the Germ thereof. But this once accomplished, that particular Complex is destroyed, or sublimated, for ever.

τ

DE MORBIS SANGUINIS

OW THEN UNDERSTAND THAT ALL OPPOsition to the Way of Nature createth Violence. If thine excretory System do its Function not at its fullest, there come Poisons in the Blood, and the Consciousness is modified by the Conflicts or Marriages between the Elements heterogeneous. Thus if the Liver be not efficient, we have Melancholy; if the Kidneys, Coma; if the Testes or Ovaries, loss of Personality itself. Also, an we poison the Blood directly with Belladonna, we have Delirium vehement and furious; with Hashish, Visions phantastic and enormous; with Anhalonium, Ecstasy of Colour and what not; with divers Germs of Disease, Disturbances of Consciousness varying with the Nature of the Germ. Also, with Ether, we gain the Power of analysing the Consciousness into its Planes and even of discovering the hidden Will and Judgment upon any Question; and so for many others.

But all these are, in our mystical Sense, Poisons; that is, we take two Things diverse and opposite, binding them together so that they are compelled to unite; and the Orgasm of each Marriage is an Ecstasy, the lower dissolving in the higher.

V

DE CURSU AMORIS

I CONTINUE THEN, O MY SON, AND REiterate that this Formula is general to all Nature. And thou wilt note that by repeated Marriage cometh Toleration, so that Ecstasy appeareth no more. Thus his half grain of Morphia, which at first opened the Gates of Heaven, is nothing worth to the Self-poisoner after a Year of daily Practice. So too the Lover findeth no more Joy in Union with his Mistress, so soon as the original Attraction between them is satisfied by repeated Conjunctions. For this Attraction is an Antagonism; and the greater the Antinomy, the more fierce the Puissance of the Magnetism, and the Quantity of Energy disengaged by the Coition. Thus in the Union of Similars, as of Halogens with each other, is no strong Passion or explosive Force; and the Love between two Persons of like Character and Taste is placid and without Transmutation to higher Planes.

φ

DE NUPTIIS MYSTICIS

MY SON, HOW WONDERFUL IS THE Wisdom of this Law of Love! How vast are the Oceans of uncharted Joy that lie before the Keel of thy Ship! Yet know this, that every Opposition is in its Nature named Sorrow, and the Joy lieth in the Destruction of the Dyad. Therefore, must thou seek ever those Things which are to thee poisonous, and that in the highest Degree, and make them thine by Love. That which repels, that which disgusts, must thou assimilate in this Way of Wholeness. Yet rest not in the Joy of the Destruction of every Complex in thy Nature, but press on to that ultimate Marriage with the Universe whose Consummation shall destroy thee utterly, leaving only that Nothingness which was before the Beginning.

So then the Life of Non-action is not for thee; the Withdrawal from Activity is not the Way of the Tao; but rather the Intensification and making universal of every Unit of thine Energy on every Plane.

χ

DE VOLUPTATE POENARUM

O FORTH, O MY SON, O SON OF THE SUN, rejoicing in thy Strength, as a Warrior, as a Bridegroom, to take thy Pleasure upon the Earth, and in every Palace of the Mind, moving ever from the crass to the subtle, from the coarse to the fine. Conquer every Repulsion in thy Self, subdue every Aversion. Assimilate all Poison, for therein only is there Profit. Seek constantly therefore to know what is painful and to cleave thereunto, for by Pain cometh true Pleasure. Those who avoid Pain physical or mental remain little Men, and there is no Virtue in them. Yet be thou ware lest thou fall into that Heresy which maketh Pain and Self-sacrifice as it were Bribes to a corrupt God, to secure some future Pleasure in an imagined After-life. Nay, also, of the other Part, fear not to destroy thy Complexes, thinking dreadfully thereby to lose the Power of creating Joy by their Distinction. Yet in each Marriage be thou bold to affirm the spiritual Ardour of the Orgasm, fixing it in some Talisman, whether it be Art, or Magick, or Theurgy.

ψ

DE VOLUNTATE ULTIMA

SAY NOT THEN THAT THIS WAY IS CONTRARY to Nature, and that in Simplicity of Satisfaction of thy Needs is Perfection of thy Path. For to thee, who hast aspired, it is thy Nature to perform the Great Work, and this is the final Dissolution of the Cosmos. For though a Stone seem to lie still on a Mountain Top, and have no Care, yet hath it an hidden Nature, a Task Ineffable and Stupendous; namely, to force its Way to the Centre of Gravity of the Universe, and also to burn up its Elements into the final Homogeneity of Matter. Therefore the Way of Quiet is but an Illusion of Ignorance. Whoever thou mayst be now, thy Destiny is that which I have declared unto thee; and thou art most fixed in the True Way when, accepting this consciously as thy Will, thou gathereth up thy Powers to move thy Self mightily within it.

ω

DE DIFFERENTIA RERUM

BUT, O MY SON, ALTHOUGH THINE ULTIMATE Nature be Universal, thine immediate Nature is Particular. Thy Way to the Centre is not oriented as that of any other Being, and thine Elements are not kin, but alien, to his. For Shame! is it not the most transcendent of all the Wisdoms of this Cosmos, that no two Beings are alike? Lo! this is the Secret of all Beauty, and maketh Love not only possible, but necessary, between every Thing and every other Thing. So then, lest thou in thine Ignorance take some false Way, and divagate, must thou learn thine own particular and peculiar Nature in its Relation to all others. For though it be Illusion, it is by the true Analysis of Falsehoods that we are able to destroy them, just as the Physician must understand the Disease of his Patient if he is to choose the fitting Remedy. Now therefore will I make yet more clear unto thee the Value of thy Dreams and Phantasies and Gestures of thine unconscious Body and Mind, as Symptoms of thy particular Will, and shew thee how thou mayst come to their Interpretation.

Aα

DE VOLUNTATE TACITA

LL DISTURBANCES, O MY SON, ARE VARIations from Equilibrium; and just as thy conscious Thoughts, Words, and Acts are Effects of the Displacement of the conscious Will, so is it in the Unconscious. For the most Part, therefore, all Dreams, Phantasies, and Gestures represent that Will subliminal; and if the physical Part of that Will be unsatisfied, its Utterance will predominate in all these automatic Expressions. Do thou then note what Modifications thereof follow such Changes in the conscious Foundation of that Part of thine Will as thou mayst make in thy Experiments therewith, and thus separate, as sayeth Trismegistus, the fine from the coarse, Fire from Earth, or, as we may say, assign each Effect to its true Cause. Seek then to perfect a conscious Satisfaction of every Part of this Will, so that the unconscious Disturbances be at last brought to Silence. Then will the Residuum be as it were an Elixir clarified and perfected, a true Symbol of that other hidden Will which is the Vector of thy Magical Self.

Aβ

DE FORMULA SUMMA

EARN MOREOVER THAT THY SELF includeth the whole Universe of thy Knowledge, so that every Increase upon every Plane is an Aggrandizement of that Self. Yet the greater part of this Universe is common Knowledge, so that thy Self is interwoven with other Selves, save for that Part peculiar to thy Self. And as thou growest, so also this peculiar Part is ever of less Proportion to the Whole, until when thou becomest infinite, it is a Quantity infinitesimal and to be neglected. Lo! when the All is absorbed within the I, it is as if the I were absorbed within the All; for if two Things become wholly and indissolubly One Thing, there is no more Reason for Names, since Names are given to mark off one Thing from another. And this is that which is written in *The Book of the Law*: "Let there be no difference made among you between any one thing & any other thing; for thereby there cometh hurt. But whoso availeth in this, let him be the chief of all!"

Aγ

De Via Inertiae

OF THE WAY OF THE TAO I HAVE ALREADY written to thee, o my Son, but I must further instruct thee in this Doctrine of doing Everything by doing Nothing. I will first have thee to understand that the Universe being as above said an Expression of Zero under the Figure of the Dyad, its Tendency is continually to release itself from that Strain by the Marriage of Opposites whenever they are brought into Contact. Thus thy true Nature is a Will to Zero, or an Inertia, or Doing Nothing; and the Way of Doing Nothing is to oppose no Obstacle to the free Function of that true Nature. Consider the Electrical Charge of a Cloud, whose Will is to discharge itself in Earth, and so to release the Strain of its Potential. Do this by free Conduction, there is Silence and Darkness; oppose it, there is Heat and Light, and the Rending asunder of that which will not permit free Passage to the Current.

Aδ

DE VIA LIBERTATIS

O NOT THINK THEN THAT BY NON-ACTION thou dost follow the Way of the Tao, for thy Nature is Action, and by hindering the Discharge of thy Potential thou dost perpetuate and aggravate the Stress. If thou ease not Nature, she will bring thee to Dis-ease. Free therefore every Function of thy Body and of every other Part of thee according to its True Will. This also is most necessary, that thou discover that True Will in every Case, for thou art born into Dis-ease; where are many false and perverted Wills, monstrous Growths, Parasites, Vermin are they, adherent to thee by Vice of Heredity or of Environment or of evil Training. And of all these Things the subtlest and most terrible, Enemies without Pity, destructive to thy Will, and a Menace and Tyranny even to thy Self, are the Ideals and Standards of the Slave-Gods, false Religion, false Ethics, even false Science.

Aε

De Lege Motus

onsider, my Son, that Word in the Call or Key of the Thirty Æthyrs: Behold the Face of your God, the Beginning of Comfort, whose Eyes are the Brightness of the Heavens, which provided you for the Government of the Earth, and her Unspeakable Variety! And again: Let there be no Creature upon her or within her the same. All her Members let them differ in their Qualities, and let there be no Creature equal with another. Here also is the Voice of true Science, crying aloud: Variation is the Key of Evolution. Thereunto Art cometh the third, perceiving Beauty in the Harmony of the Diverse. Know then, o my Son, that all Laws, all Systems, all Customs, all Ideals and Standards which tend to produce Uniformity, being in direct Opposition to Nature's Will to change and to develop through Variety, are accurséd. Do thou with all thy Might of Manhood strive against these Forces, for they resist Change, which is Life; and thus they are of Death.

On the Law of Motion

AF

DE LEGIBUS CONTRA MOTUM

SAY NOT, IN THINE HASTE, THAT SUCH Stagnations are Unity even as the last Victory of thy free Will is Unity. For thy Will moveth through free Function, according to its particular Nature, to that End of Dissolution of all Complexities, and the Ideals and Standards are Attempts to halt thee on that Way. Although for thee some certain Ideal be upon thy Path; yet for thy Neighbour it may not be so. Set all Men a-horseback: thou speedest the Foot-soldier upon his Way, indeed; but what hast thou done to the Bird-man? Thou must have simple Laws and Customs to express the general Will, and so prevent the Tyranny or Violence of a few; but multiply them not! Now then herewith I will declare unto thee the Limits of the Civil Law upon the Rock of the Law of Thelema.

 On the Laws against Motion

Aζ

De Necessitate Communi

NDERSTAND FIRST THAT THE DISTURBERS of the Peace of Mankind do so by Reason of their Ignorance of their own True Wills. Therefore, as this Wisdom of mine increaseth among Mankind, the false Will to Crime must become constantly more rare. Also, the Exercise of our Freedom will cause Men to be born with less and ever less Affliction from that Dis-ease of Spirit, which breedeth these false Wills. But, in the While of waiting for this Perfection, thou must by Law assure to every Man a Means of satisfying his bodily and his mental Needs, leaving him free to develop any Superstructure in accordance with his Will, and protecting him from any that may seek to deprive him of these vertebral Rights. There shall be therefore a Standard of Satisfaction, though it must vary in Detail with Race, Climate, and other such Conditions. And this Standard shall be based upon a large Interpretation of Facts biological, physiological, and the like.

On the Common Need

An

De Libertate Corporis

There shall be no Property in Human Flesh. Every Man and every Woman hath *Right Indefeasable* to give the Body for the Enjoyment of any other. The Exercise of that Right shall not be punished either by Law or by Custom; there shall be no Penalty either by Loss or Curtailment of Liberty, of Rights, of Wealth, or of social Esteem; but this Freedom shall be respected of all, seeing that it is the Right of the bodily Will. For this same Reason thou shalt cause full Restriction and Punishment of any who may seek to limit that Freedom for the sake of his own Profit, or Desire, or Ideal. Every Man and every Woman hath full right either to grant or to deny the Body, as the Will speaketh within. This being made Custom, the Evils of Love, which are many, extending to the Disturbance not only of Body but of Mind, and that in obscure Paths, shall little by little disappear from the Face of His unspeakable Glory.

Aθ

DE LIBERTATE MENTIS

HERE SHALL BE NO PROPERTY IN HUMAN Thought. Let each think as he will concerning the Universe; but let none seek to impose that Thought upon another by any Threat of Penalty in this World or any other World. Look now, though I enkindle thee to Effort in thy Way, yet it is the Way of thy Will, and I say not even that thou dost well to haste therein, for the whole Matter lieth in thy Will, and to force thyself against thy Nature would be an Obstacle to thy Passage. But if I urge thee to run well this Race as an Athlete, it is because I have perceived in thy Nature that fierce Lust and mighty Concentration in that Will, and I write this Letter unto thee knowing well that thou wilt rejoice exceedingly therein, since it is an Expression of thine own Will, and it may be a Discovery thereof, which Thing thou vehemently seekest. I charge thee therefore that thou permit none to tyrannize any other in Thought, or to threaten, or in any other wise to blaspheme the great Liberty of Our Father the Sun in the Great Cosmos, or of His Viceregent in the Little.

AL

DE LIBERATATE IUVENUM

THOU THAT ART THE CHILD OF MINE OWN Bowels, how shall I write to thee concerning Children? For herein is the Gordian Knot in our whole Rope of Wisdom, and it may not be severed by Sword, no, not of a greater than Alexander the Two-Horned. And it is a Balance like that of the Egg, and the Violence of a Columbus will but crack the tender Shell which we must first of all preserve.

Now Sentinel to this Fortress standeth a certain Paradox of general Application, and in this large Order I will declare it, so that its particular Sense may enlighten thy Mind hereafter. And this is the Paradox, that there are Bonds which lead to Slavery, and Bonds which lead to Freedom. All we are bound in many Fetters by Environment, and it is for ourselves in great Part to determine whether they shall enslave us or emancipate us. And I will make clear this Thesis to thee by the Way of Illustration.

AK

DE VI PER DISCIPLINAM COLENDA

ONSIDER THE BOND OF A COLD CLIMATE, how it maketh Man a Slave: he must have Shelter and Food with fierce Toil. Yet thereby he becometh strong against the Elements, and his moral Force waxeth, so that he is Master of such Men as live in Lands of Sun where bodily Needs are satisfied without Struggle.

Consider also him that willeth to excel in Speed or in Battle, how he denieth himself the Food he craveth, and all Pleasures natural to him, putting himself under the harsh Order of a Trainer. So by this Bondage he hath, at the last, his Will.

Now then the one by natural, and the other by voluntary, Restriction have come each to greater Liberty. This is also a general Law of Biology, for all Development is Structuralization; that is, a Limitation and Specialization of an originally indeterminate Protoplasm, which latter may therefore be called free, in the Definition of a Pedant.

Aλ

DE ORDINE RERUM

N THE BODY EVERY CELL IS SUBORDINATED to the general physiological Control, and we who will that Control do not ask whether each individual Unit of that Structure be consciously happy. But we do care that each shall fulfil its Function, and the Failure of even a few Cells, or their Revolt, may involve the Death of the whole Organism. Yet even here the Complaint of a few, which we call Pain, is a Warning of general Danger. Many Cells fulfil their Destiny by swift Death, and this being their Function, they in no wise resent it. Should Hæmoglobin resist the Attack of Oxygen, the Body would perish, and the Hæmoglobin would not thereby save itself. Now, o my Son, do then consider deeply of these Things in thine Ordering of the World under the Law of Thelema. For every Individual in the State must be perfect in his own Function, with Contentment, respecting his own Task as necessary and holy, not envious of another's. For so only mayst thou build up a Free State, whose directing Will shall be singly directed to the Welfare of all.

Aμ

DE FUNDAMENTIS CIVITATIS

SAY NOT, O MY SON, THAT IN THIS ARGUMENT I have set Limits to individual Freedom. For each Man in this State which I purpose is fulfilling his own True Will by his eager Acquiescence in the Order necessary to the Welfare of all, and therefore of himself also. But see thou well to it that thou set high the Standard of Satisfaction, and that to every one be a Surplus of Leisure and of Energy, so that, his Will of Self-preservation being fulfilled by the Performance of his Function in the State, he may devote the Remainder of his Powers to the Satisfaction of the other Parts of his Will. And because the People are oft-times unlearned, not understanding Pleasure, let them be instructed in the Art of Life: to prepare Food palatable and wholesome, each to his own Taste, to make Clothes according to Fancy, with Variety of Individuality, and to practice the manifold Crafts of Love. These Things being first secured, thou mayst afterward lead them into the Heavens of Poesy and Tale, of Music, Painting, and Sculpture, and into the Lore of the Mind itself, with its insatiable Joy of all Knowledge. Thence let them soar!

On the Fundamentals of the State

AV

DE VOLUNTATE IUVENUM

ONG, O MY SON, HATH BEEN THIS DIGRESSION from the plain Path of my Word concerning Children; but it was most needful that thou shouldst understand the Limits of true Liberty. For that is not the Will of any Man which ultimateth in his own Ruin and that of all his Fellows; and that is not Liberty whose Exercise bringeth him to Bondage. Thou mayst therefore assume that it is alway an essential Part of the Will of any Child to grow to Manhood or to Womanhood in Health, and his Guardians may therefore prevent him from ignorantly acting in Opposition thereunto, Care being always taken to remove the Cause of the Error, namely, Ignorance, as aforesaid. Thou mayst also assume that it is Part of the Child's Will to train every Function of the Mind; and the Guardians may therefore combat the Inertia which hinders its Development. Yet here is much Caution necessary, and it is better to work by exciting and satisfying any natural Curiosity than by forcing Application to set Tasks, however obvious this Necessity may appear.

Aξ

DE MODO DISPUTANDI

OW IN THIS TRAINING OF THE CHILD IS one most dear Consideration, that I shall impress upon thee as in Conformity with our holy Experience in the Way of Truth. And it is this, that since that which can be thought is not true, every Statement is in some Sense false. Even on the Sea of pure Reason, we may say that every Statement is in some Sense disputable. Therefore in every Case, even the simplest, the Child should be taught not only the Thesis, but also its Opposite, leaving the Decision to the Child's own Judgment and good Sense, fortified by Experience. And this Practice will develop its Power of Thought, and its Confidence in itself, and its Interest in all Knowledge. But most of all be ware against any Attempt to bias its Mind on any Point that lieth without the Square of ascertained and undisputed Fact. Remember also, even when thou art most sure, that so were they sure who gave Instruction to the young Copernicus. Pay Reverence also to the Unknown unto whom thou presumest to impart thy Knowledge; for he may be one greater than thou.

On the Method of Argument

Ao

DE VOLUNTATE IUVENIS COGNOSCENDA

T IS IMPORTANT THAT THOU SHOULDST understand as early as may be what is the True Will of the Child in the Matter of his Career. Be thou well ware of all Ideals and Day-dreams; for the Child is himself, and not thy Toy. Recall the comic Tragedy of Napoleon and the King of Rome; build not an House for a wild Goat, nor plant a Forest for the Domain of a Shark. But be thou vigilant for every Sign, conscious or unconscious, of the Will of the Child, giving him then all Opportunity to pursue the Path which he thus indicates. Learn this, that he, being young, will weary quickly of all false Ways, however pleasant they may be to him at the Outset; but of the true Way he will not weary. This being in this Manner discovered, thou mayst prepare it for him perfectly; for no Man can keep all Roads open for ever. And to him making his Choice, explain how one may not travel far on any one Road without a general Knowledge of Things apparently irrelevant. And with that he will understand, and bend him wisely to his Work.

Aπ

DE AURO RUBEO

I WOULD HAVE THEE TO CONSIDER, O MY Son, that Word of Publius Vergilius Maro, that was the greatest of all the Magicians of his Time: *in medio tutissimus ibis.* Which Thing hath also been said by many wise Men in other Lands; and the Holy Qabalah confirmeth the same, placing Tiphareth, which is the Man, and the Beauty and Harmony of Things, and Gold in the Kingdom of the Metals, and the Sun among the Planets, in the Midst of the Tree of Life. For the Centre is the Point of Balance of all Vectors. So then if thou wilt live wisely, learn that thou must establish this Relation of Balance with every Thing soever, not omitting one. For there is nothing so alien from thy Nature that it may not be brought into harmonious Relation therewith; and thy Stature of Manhood waxeth great even as thou comest to the Perfection of this Art. And there is nothing so close Kin to thee that it may not be hurtful to thee if this Balance be not truly adjusted. Thou hast need of the whole Force of the Universe to work with thy Will; but this Force must be disposed about the Shaft of that Will so that there is no Tendency to Hindrance or to Deflection. And in my Love of thee I will adorn this Thesis with Example following.

A♀

DE SAPIENTIA IN RE SEXUALI

CONSIDER LOVE. HERE IS A FORCE destructive and corrupting whereby many Men have been lost: witness all History. Yet without Love Man were not Man. Therefore thine Uncle Richard Wagner made of Our Doctrine a Musical Fable, wherein we see Amfortas, who yielded himself to Seduction, wounded beyond Healing; Klingsor, who withdrew himself from a like Danger, cast out for ever from the Mountain of Salvation; and Parsifal, who yielded not, able to exercise the true Power of Love, and thereby to perform the Miracle of Redemption. Of this also have I myself written in my Poema called *Adonis*. It is the same with Food and Drink, with Exercise, with Learning itself; the Problem is ever to bring the Appetite into the right Relation with the Will. Thus thou mayst fast or feast; there is no Rule, but that of Balance. And this Doctrine is of general Acceptation among the better sort of Men; therefore on thee will I rather impress more carefully the other Part of my Wisdom, namely, the Necessity of extending constantly thy Nature to new Mates upon every Plane of Being, so that thou mayst become the perfect Microcosm, an Image without Flaw of all that is.

Αρ

DE GRADIBUS AEQUIS SCIENTIAE

SAY IN SOOTH, MY SON, THAT THIS EXTENSION of thy Nature is not in Violation thereof; for it is the Nature of thy Nature to grow continually. Now there is no Part of Knowledge which is foreign to thee; yet Knowledge itself is of no avail unless it be assimilated and co-ordinated into Understanding. Grow therefore easily and spontaneously, developing all Parts equally, lest thou become a Monster. And if one Thing tempt thee overmuch, correct it by Devotion to its Opposite until Equilibrium be re-established. But seek not to grow by sudden Determination toward Things that be far from thee; only, if such a Thing come into thy Thought, construct a Bridge thereunto, and take firmly the first Step upon that Bridge. I shall explain this. Dost thou speculate upon the Motives of the Stars, and on their Elements, their Size and Weight? Then thou must first gain Knowledge of Things mathematical, of Laws physical and chemical. So then first, that thou mayst understand clearly the Nature of thine whole Work, map out thy Mind, and extend its Powers from the essential outwards, from the near to the far, always with Firmness and great Thoroughness, making every Link in thy Chain equal and perfect.

Aσ

DE VIRTUTE AUDENDI

ET THIS I CHARGE THEE WITH MY MIGHT: Live Dangerously. Was not this the Word of thine Uncle Friedrich Nietzsche? Thy meanest Foe is the Inertia of the Mind. Men do hate most those Things which touch them closely, and they fear Light, and persecute the Torchbearers. Do thou therefore analyse most fully all those Ideas which Men avoid; for the Truth shall dissolve Fear. Rightly indeed Men say that the Unknown is terrible; but wrongly do they fear lest it become the Known. Moreover, do thou all Acts of which the common Sort beware, save where thou hast already full Knowledge, that thou mayst learn Use and Control, not falling into Abuse and Slavery. For the Coward and the Foolhardy shall not live out their Days. Every Thing has his right Use; and thou art great as thou hast Use of Things. This is the Mystery of all Art Magick, and thine Hold upon the Universe. Yet if thou must err, being human, err by excess of Courage rather than of Caution; for it is the Foundation of the Honour of Man that he dareth greatly. What saith Quintus Horatius Flaccus in the third Ode of his First Book? Die thou standing!

Aτ

DE ARTE MENTIS COLENDI

(1) MATHEMATICA

OW, CONCERNING THE FIRST FOUNDATION of thy Mind I will say somewhat. Thou shalt study with Diligence in the Mathematics, because thereby shall be revealed unto thee the Laws of thine own Reason and the Limitations thereof. This Science manifesteth unto thee thy true Nature in respect of the Machinery whereby it worketh, and showeth in pure Nakedness, without Clothing of Personality or Desire, the Anatomy of thy conscious Self. Furthermore, by this thou mayst understand the Essence of the Relations between all Things, and the Nature of Necessity, and come to the Knowledge of Form. For this Mathematics is as it were the last Veil before the Image of Truth, so that there is no Way better than our Holy Qabalah, which analyseth all Things soever, and reduceth them to pure Number; and thus their Natures being no longer coloured and confused, they may be regulated and formulated in Simplicity by the Operation of Pure Reason, to thy great Comfort in the Work of our Transcendental Art, whereby the Many become One.

On the Art of Training the Mind. (1) Mathematics.

Ad

Sequitur

(2) Classica

y Son, neglect not in any wise the study of the Writings of Antiquity, and that in the original Language. For by this thou shalt discover the History of the Structure of thy Mind, that is, its Nature regarded as the last Term in a Sequence of Causes and Effects. For thy Mind hath been built up of these Elements, so that in these Books thou mayst bring into the Light thine own subconscious Memories. And thy Memory is as it were the Mortar in the House of thy Mind, without which is no Cohesion or Individuality possible, so that it is called Dementia. And these Books have lived long and become famous because they are the Fruits of ancient Trees whereof thou art directly the Heir, wherefore (say I) they are more truly german to thine own Nature than Books of Collateral Offshoots, though such were in themselves better and wiser. Yea, o my Son, in these Writings thou mayst study to come to the true Comprehension of thine own Nature, and that of the whole Universe, in the Dimension of Time, even as the Mathematic declareth it in that of Space: that is, of Extension. Moreover, by this Study shall the Child comprehend the Foundation of Manners: the which, as sayeth one of the Sons of Wisdom, maketh Man.

 Continued.
(2) Classics

Aφ

SEQUITUR

(3) SCIENTIFICA

INCE TIME AND SPACE ARE THE Conditions of Mind, these two Studies are fundamental. Yet there remaineth Causality, which is the Root of the Actions and Reactions of Nature. This also shalt thou seek ardently, that thou mayst comprehend the Variety of the Universe, its Harmony and its Beauty, with the Knowledge of that which compelleth it. Yet this is not equal to the former two in Power to reveal thee to thyself; and its first Use is to instruct thee in the true Method of Advancement in Knowledge, which is, fundamentally, the Observation of the Like and the Unlike. Also, it shall arouse in thee the Ecstasy of Wonder; and it shall bring thee to a proper Understanding of Art Magick. For our Magick is but one of the Powers that lie within us undeveloped and unanalysed; and it is by the Method of Science that it must be made clear, and available to the Use of Man. Is not this a Gift beyond Price, the Fruit of a Tree not only of Knowledge but of Life? For there is that in Man which is God, and there is that also which is Dust; and by our Magick we shall make these twain one Flesh, to the Obtaining of the Empery of the Universe.

Continued.
(3) Science

Aχ

De Modo Quo Operet Lex Magica

IVE EAR ATTENTIVELY, O MY SON, WHILE I expound unto thee the true Doctrine of Magick. Every Force acteth, in due Proportion, on all Things with which it is connected. Thus a burning Forest causeth chemical Change by Combustion, and giveth Heat and Motion to the Air about it by the Operation of physical Laws, and exciteth Thought and Emotion in the Man whom it reacheth through his Organs of Perception. Consider (even though it were but Legend) the Fall of the Apple of Isaac Newton, its Effect upon the Spiritual Destinies of Man! Consider also that no Force cometh ever to the End of its Work; the Air that is moved by my Breath is a Disturbance or Change of Equilibrium that cannot be fully compensated and brought to naught, though the Æons be endless. Who then shall deny the Possibility of Magick? Well said Frazer, the most learned Doctor of the College of the Holy Trinity in the University of Cambridge, that Science was but the Name of Magick which failed not of its intended Effect.

Aψ

DE MACHINA MAGICA

o! I PUT FORTH MY WILL, AND MY PEN moveth upon the Paper, by cause that my Will mysteriously hath Power upon the Muscles of my Arm, and these do Work at a mechanical Advantage against the Inertia of the Pen. I cannot break down the Wall opposite me, by cause that I cannot come into mechanical Relation with it; or the Wall at my Side, by cause that I am not strong enough to overcome its Inertia. To win that Battle I must call Time and Pick-axe to mine Aid. But how could I retard the Motion of the Earth in Space? I am myself Party of its Momentum. Yet every Stroke of my Pen affecteth that Motion by changing the Equilibrium thereof. The Problem of every Act of Magick is then this: to exert a Will, sufficiently powerful to cause the required Effect, through a Menstruum or Medium of Communication. By the common Understanding of the word Magick, we yet exclude such Media as are generally known and understood. Now then, o my Son, will I declare unto thee first the Nature of the Power, and afterward that of the Medium.

On the Mechanism of Magick

Aω

DE HARMONIA ANIMAE CUM CORPORE

LL THINGS ARE INTERWOVEN. THE MOST spiritual Thought in thy Soul (I speak as a Fool) is also a most material Change in Blood or Brain. Anger maketh the Blood acid; Hate poisoneth Mother's Milk; even as I shewed formerly in reverse, how Disturbance of physical Function altereth the States of Consciousness. Now no Man doubteth the Power of the Will of Man, whether it be his Love that begetteth Children or causeth Wars wherein many Men be slain, whether it be his Eloquence that moveth a Mob, or his Vanity that destroyeth a People. Only in all such Cases we understand how Nature worketh, through known Laws physical or psychical. That is, there is a State of unstable Equilibrium, so that one Machine setteth another in Motion as soon as the first Disturbance ariseth. Therefore, it is not proper to regard all Consequence of a Will as its Effect. Without the Revolution there could have been no great Effect of the Will of Napoleon; and moreover his Will was broken in the End, to the present Misfortune (as it seemeth to many besides myself) of Mankind. This Magick, therefore, dependeth greatly on the Art to set many other Wills in sympathetic Motion; and the greatest Magus may not be the most successful — in a mean Conception of a Limit of Time. He may need many Blows before he breaketh down his Wall, if that be strong, while a Child may push over one that is ready to crumble.

Bα

DE MYSTERIO PRUDENTIAE

EHOLD NOW NATURE, HOW PRODIGAL IS She of her Forces! The evident Will of every Acorn is to become an Oak; yet nigh all fail of that Will. Therefore one Secret of Magick is Œconomy of thy Force; to do no Act unless secure of its Effect. And if every Act hath an Effect on every Plane, how canst thou do this unless thou be connected with all Planes? For this Reason must thou know thoroughly not only thy Body and thy Mind, but thy Body of Light and all its subtler Principles soever. But I will have thee to consider most especially what Powers thou hast within thee which are certainly capable of great Effects, yet which are constantly wasted. Think then whether if these Powers, frustrate of their End upon one Plane, might not be turned to high Purpose and assured Success upon another. For an hundred Acorns, rightly set in Conditions fit for their true Growth, will become an hundred Oaks, while otherwise they make but one Meal for one Hog, and their subtile Nature is wholly lost to them. Learn then, o my Son, this Mystery of Œconomy, and apply it faithfully and with Diligence in thy Work.

Bβ

DE ARTE ALCHEMICA

HERE THEN MUST I WRITE CONCERNING Talismans for thine Instruction. Know first that there are certain Vehicles proper for the Incarnation of the Will. I instance Paper, whereon by thine Art thou writest a symbolic Representation of thy Will, so that when thou next seest it, thou are reminded of that Will, or it may be that another, seeing it, is moved to obey that Will. Here then is a case of Incarnation and Assumption, which, before it was understood, was rightly considered Gramarye or Magick. Again, thy Will to live causeth thee to plant Corn, which in due Season being eaten is again transmuted into Will. Thus thou mayst in many Ways impress any particular Will upon the proper Substance, so that by due Use thou comest at last to its Accomplishment. So general is this Formula, in Truth, that all conscious Actions may be included within its Scope. There is also the Converse, as when external Objects create Appetite, whose Satisfaction again reacteth upon the physical Plane. Praise thou the wonder of the Mystery of Nature, rising and falling with every Breath, so that there is no Part which is not mystically Partaker of the Whole.

Bγ

DE ARCANO SUBTILISSIMO

MY SON, THERE IS THAT WITHIN THEE of marvellous Puissance which is by its own Nature the Incarnation of thy Will, most ready to receive the Seal thereof. Therein lie hidden all Powers, all Memories, more than thou hast thyself ten thousandfold! Learn then to draw from that great Treasure-House the Jewel of which thou art in any present Need. For all Things that are possible to thy Nature are already hidden within thee; and thou hast but to name them, and to bring them back into the Light of thy Consciousness. Then squander not this Gold of thine, but put it to most fruitful Usury. Now then of the Art and Craft of this most holy Mystery I write not, for a Reason that thou already knowest. Moreover, in this Matter thou shalt best learn by thine own Experience, and thine Observation in true Science shall guide thee. For this Secret is still of Magick, and occult, so that I know not certainly if thy Will lieth my Way or no.

Bδ

DE MENSTRUO ARTIS

UT CONCERNING THE MEDIUM BY WHOSE sensitive Nature our Magick Force is transmitted to the Object of our Working, doubt not. For already in other Galaxies of Physics have some been compelled to postulate an Æthyr wholly hypothetical in order to explain the Phenomena of Light, Electricity, and the like; nor doth any Man demand Demonstration of the Existence of that Æthyr other than its Conformity with general Law. Thou therefore, Creator and Transmitter of thine own Energy, needest not to ask whether by this or by some other Means thou performest thy Work. Yet I know not why this Æthyr which the Mathematicians and the Physicists imagined, yet were not able to define, its Nature being beyond Reason, should not be one with the Astral Light, or Plastic Medium, or Aub, Aud, Aur (these three being a Trinity) of which our own Sages have spoken. And this Meditation may bring forth much Knowledge physical, which is good, for that which is above is like that which is beneath, and the Study of any Law leadeth to the Understanding of all Law. So mayst thou learn in the End that there is no Law beyond Do what thou wilt.

56 ❧ *On the Medium of the Art*

Bε

De Necessitate Voluntatis

ND HOW THEN (SAYST THOU?) SHALL I reconcile this Art Magick with that Way of the Tao which achieveth all Things by doing Nothing? But this have I already declared to thee in Part, shewing that thou canst do no Magick save it be thy Nature to do Magick, and so the true Nothing for thee. For to do Nothing signifieth to interfere with Nothing, so that for a Magician to do no Magick is to commit Violence on himself. Yet learn also that all Action is in some sense Magick, being an essential Part of that Great Magical Work which we call Nature. Then thou hast no Free Will? Verily, thou hast said. Yet never the less it is thy necessary Destiny to act with that Free Will. Thou canst do nothing save in accordance with that Nature of thine and of all Things, and every Phenomenon is the Resultant of the Totality of Forces: Amen. Then thou needst take no Thought and make no Effort? Thou sayest sooth; yet, art thou not compelled to Thought and Effort in the Way of Nature? Yea, I, thy Father, work for thee solicitously, and also I laugh at thy Perplexities; for so was it foreordained that I should do, by Me, from the Beginning.

On the Necessity of the Will

BF

DE COMEDIA UNIVERSA, QUAE DICITUR ΠAN

O, THEREFORE, O MY SON, COUNT THYSELF happy when thou understandest all these Things, being one of those Beings (or By-comings) whom we call Philosophers. All is a never-ending Play of Love wherein Our Lady Nuit and Her Lord Hadit rejoice; and every Part of the Play is Play. All Pain is but sharp Sauce to the Dish of Pleasure; for it is the Nature of the Universe that hath devised this everlasting Banquet of Joy. And he that knoweth not this is necessary as an Ingredient even as thou art; wouldst thou change all, and spoil the Dish? Art thou the Master-Cook? Yea, for thy Palate is become fine with thy great Dalliance with the Food of Experience; therefore thou art one of them that rejoice. Also it is thy Nature as it is mine, o my Son, to will that all Men share our Mirth and Jollity; wherefore have I proclaimed my Law to Man, and thou continuest in that Work of Joyaunce.

Bζ

DE CAECITIA HOMINUM

EARN ALSO OF MY WISDOM THAT THIS Vision of the Cosmos whereof I have here written unto thee is not given unto thy Sight at all Times; for in that Vision is all Will fulfilled. Thou seest the Universe as None, and as One, and as Many, and thou seest the Play thereof; and therewith art thou (who art no longer thou) content. For in one Phase art thou also None, in another One, and in the third an organized and necessary Part of that great Structure, so that there is no more Conflict at all in thy whole By-coming. But now will I make Light for thine Eyes in this Matter as thou gropest, asking: but of them that see not this, what sayst thou, o my Father? But in that Vision thou sayst not thus, my Son! Learn then of me the Secret Mystery of Illusion, and how it worketh, and of the Holy Law that is its Nature, and of thine Action therein; for this is an Arcanum of the Wisdom of the Magi, and proper unto thee that dwellest in the Land of Understanding.

On the Blindness of Men

Bη

ALLEGORIA DE CAISSA

ONSIDER FOR AN EXAMPLE THE GAME and Play of the Chess, which is a Pastime of Man, and worthy to exercise him in Thought, yet by no means necessary to his Life, so that he sweepeth away Board and Pieces at the least Summons of that which is truly dear to him. Thus unto him this Game is as it were an Illusion. But insofar as he entereth into the Game he abideth by the Rules thereof, though they be of Artifice and in no wise proper to his Nature; for in this Restriction is all his Pleasure. Therefore, though he hath All-Power to move the Pieces at his own Will, he doth it not, enduring Loss, Indignity, and Defeat rather than destroy that Artifice of Illusion. Think then that thou hast thyself created this Shadow-world the Universe, and that it pleasureth thee to watch or to actuate its Play according to the Law that thou hast made, which yet bindeth thee not save only by Virtue of thine own Will to thine own Pleasure therein.

Bθ

De Veritate Falsi

OREOVER THIS MATTER TOUCHETH THE Nature of Truth. For although to thee in thy True Self, absolute and without Conditions, all this Universe, which is relative and conditioned, is an Illusion; yet to that Part of thee by which thou perceivest it, the Law of its Being (or By-coming) is a Law of Truth. Learn then that all Relations are true upon their own Plane, and that it would be a Violation of Nature to adjust them skew-wise. Thus, albeit thou hast found Thy Self, and knowest Thy Self immortal and immutable, beyond Time and Space, free of Causality, so thoroughly that even thy Mind partaketh constantly thereof, thou hast in no wise altered the Relations of thy Body with its Syndromics in the World whereof it is a Part. Wouldst thou lengthen the Life of thy Body? Then accommodate thou the Conditions of thy Body to its Environment by giving it Light, Air, Food, and Exercise as its Nature requireth. So also, *mutatis mutandis*, do thou cherish the Health of thy Mind.

Bι

De Relatione Illusionium

F THIS WILL I SPEAK FURTHER WITH THEE, for here behold a great Rock of Ignorance on the one Hand, and on the other a Whirlpool of Error; in this Strait are many Wrecks of Magick Ships. Knowest thou not that Riddle of old, whether it be lawful to pay Tribute to Cæsar or no? Give therefore to the Body the Things of the Body, and to the Mind the Things of the Mind. Yet because of the Interior Harmony of all Things that proceedeth from their Original One Nature, there is Action and Reaction of the one upon the other, as I have already set forth in this mine Epistle. But Law is universal, and between these two Kinds of Illusion there is an ordered Proportion, and it is proper to thy Science to delimit and describe this Law of Interaction, for to deny it wholly (as to extend it to Infinity) is Folly, born of Ignorance, Idleness, and Incapacity to observe Fact.

Bκ

De Prudentia

Consider Drunkenness, how by Variation of bodily Conditions thou mayst alter its Effect upon the Mind, and the contrary, remembering the Discipline of Theophrastus Paracelsus, how, opposing Wine to bodily Exercise, he obtained a certain Purification and Exaltation. Yet, were he seven times greater, he had not done this with Oil of Vitriol. Learn then that there are certain definite Channels of Action and Reaction between Body and Mind; sound these, and trim thy Sails accordingly, not thinking that thou art in the open Sea. And if so be that thou in thy sounding findest new Channels, rejoice, and map them for the Profit of thy Fellows; But remember constantly that to find one new Way up a Precipice removeth not the Precipice. For where thou, o Angel and yet Man, hast trod delicately albeit without Fear, Fools will rush in to their Destruction.

Bλ

DE RATIONE MAGI VITAE

TUDY THOU LOGIC, WHICH IS THE CODE OF the Laws of Thought. Study the Method of Science, which is the Application of Logic to the Facts of the Universe. Think not that thou canst ever abrogate these Laws, for though they be Limitations, they are the Rules of thy Game which thou dost play. For in thy Trances though thou becomest That which is not subject to those Laws, they are still final in respect of those Things which thou hast set them to govern. Nay, o my Son, this Word govern, liketh me not, for a Law is but a Statement of the Nature of the Thing to which it applieth. For nothing is compelled save only by Virtue of its own True Will. So therefore human Law is a Statement of the Will and of the Nature of Man, or else it is a Falsity contrary thereunto, and becometh null and of none Effect.

Bμ

DE CORDE CANDIDO

HINK ALSO, O MY SON, OF THIS IMAGE, THAT if two States be at Peace, a Man goeth between them without let; but if there be War, all Gateways are forthwith closed, save only for a few, and these are watched and guarded, so that the Obstacles are many. This then is the case of Magick; for if thou have brought to Harmony all Principles within thee, thou mayst work easily to transmute a Force into its semblable upon another Plane, which is the essential Opus of our Art; but if thou be at War within thyself, how canst thou work? For our Master Hermes Trismegistus hath written at the Head of his Tablet of Emerald this Word: That which is above is like that which is below, and that which is below is like that which is above, for the Performance of the Miracles of the One Substance. How then, if these be not alike? If the Substance of Thee be Two, and not One? And herein is the Need of the Confession of a Pure Heart, as is written in the Papyrus of the Dead.

Bv

DE CONFORMITATE MAGI

EE TO IT THEREFORE, O MY SON, THAT thou in thy Working dost no Violence to the Whole Will of the All, or to the Will common to all those Beings (or By-comings) that are of one general Nature with thee, or to thine own particular Will. For first of all thou art necessarily moved toward the One End from thine own Station, but secondly thou art moved toward the End proper to thine own Race, and Caste, and Family, as by Virtue of thy Birth. And these are, I may say it, Conditions or Limits of thine own individual Will. Thou dost laugh? What, sayest thou, of the Revolutionary Will? Err not, my Son! The Magus, even as the Poet, is the Expression of the True Will of his Fellows, and his Success is his Proof, as it is written in *The Book of the Law.* For his Work is to free Men from the Fetters of a false or superannuated Will, revealing to them, in Measure attuned to their present Needs, their true Natures.

Bξ

De Poetis

FOR THIS REASON IS THE POET CALLED AN Incarnation of the Zeitgeist, that is, of the Spirit or Will of his Period. So every Poet is also a Prophet, because when that which he sayeth is recognized as the Expression of their own Thought by Men, they translate this into Act, so that, in the Parlance of Folk vulgar and ignorant, "that which he foretold is come to pass." Now then the Poet is Interpreter of the Hieroglyphs of the Hidden Will of Man in many a Matter, some light, some deep, as it may be given unto him to do. Moreover, it is not altogether in the Word of any Poem, but in the quintessential Flavour of the Poet, that thou mayst seek this Prophecy. And this is an Art most necessary to every Statesman. Who but Shelley foretold the Fall of Christianity, and the Organization of Labour, and the Freedom of Woman; who but Nietzsche declared the Principle at the Root of the World-War? See thou clearly then that in these Men were the Keys of the dark Gates of the Future; should not the Kings and their Ministers have taken heed thereto, fulfilling their Word without Conflict?

80

DE MAGIS ORDINIS A∴ A∴ QUIBUS CARO FIT VERBUM

NOW, O MY SON, THE INCARNATION OF A POET is particular and not Universal; he sayeth indeed true Things, but not the Things of All-Truth. And that these may be said it is necessary that One take human Flesh, and become a Magus in Our Holy Order. He then is called the Logos, or *Logos Aionos*, that is to say, the Word of the Æon or Age, because He is verily That Word. And thus may He be known, because He hath it given unto Him to prepare the Quintessence of the Will of God, that is, of Man, in its Fullness and Wholeness, comprehending all Planes; so that His Law is simple, and radical, penetrating all Space from its single Light. For though His Words be many, yet is His Word One, One and Alone; and by this Word he createth Man anew, in an Essential Form of Life, so that he is changed in his inmost Knowledge of himself. And this Change worketh outwards, little by little, unto its visible Effects.

Bπ

DE MAGIS TEMPORIS ANTIQUI IMPRIMIS DE LAO-TZE

T MAY BE UNTO THY PROFIT, O MY SON, if I relate unto thee the secret History of those who have gone before me in this Grade of Magus, so far as Their Memory hath remained among Mankind. For what would it avail thee should I recount the deeds of Those whom I indeed may know, but thou not? Thou knowest well how I keep me from all Taint of Fable, or of any Word unproven or undemonstrable. First then I speak of Lao-tze, whose Word was TAO. Hereof have I already written much unto thee, because His Doctrine hath been lost or misinterpreted, and it is most needful to restore it. For this Tao is the true Nature of Things, being itself a Way or Going, that is, a kinetic and not a static Conception. Also He taught this Way of Harmony in Will, which I myself have sought to shew thee in this Epistle. So then this Tao is Truth, and the Way of Truth, and therefore was Lao-tze Logos of His Æon, and His true Word or Name was TAO.

B♀

DE GAUTAMA

WHOM MEN CALL GAUTAMA, OR SIDDARTHA, or The Buddha, was a Magus of Our Holy Order. And His Word was ANATTA; for the Root of His whole Doctrine was that there is no Atman, or Soul, as Men ill translate it, meaning a Substance incapable of Change. Thus He, like Lao-tze, based all upon a Movement, instead of a fixed Point. And His Way of Truth was Analysis, made possible by great Intention of the Mind toward itself, and that well fortified by a certain tempered Rigour of Life. And He most thoroughly explored and mapped out the Fastnesses of the Mind, and gave the Keys of its Fortresses into the Hands of Man. But of all this the Quintessence is in this one Word ANATTA, because this is not only the Foundation and the Result of His whole Doctrine, but the Way of its Work.

Bρ

DE SRI KRISHNA ET DE DIONYSO

RISHNA HATH NAMES AND FORMS INNUMERABLE, and I know not His true human Birth. For His Formula is of the major Antiquity. But His Word hath spread into many Lands, and we know it to-day as INRI with the secret IAO concealed therein. And the Meaning of this Word is the Way of the Working of Nature in Her Changes; that is, it is the Formula of Magick whereby all Things reproduce and recreate themselves. Yet this Extension and Specialization was rather the Word of Dionysus; for the true Word of Krishna was AUM, importing rather a Statement of the Truth of Nature than a practical Instruction in detailed Operations of Magick. But Dionysus, by the Word INRI, laid the Foundations of all Science, as we say Science to-day in a particular Sense, that is, of causing external Nature to change in Harmony with our Wills.

On Sri Krishna and Dionysus

Βσ

De Tahuti

Tahuti, or Thoth, confirmed the Word of Dionysus by continuing it; for He shewed how by the Mind it was possible to direct the Operations of the Will. By Criticism and by recorded Memory Man avoideth Error, and the Repetition of Error. But the true Word of Tahuti was AMOUN, whereby He made Men to understand their secret Nature, that is, their Unity with their True Selves, or, as they then phrased it, with God. And He discovered unto them the Way of this Attainment, and its Relation with the Formula of INRI. Also by His Mystery of Number He made plain the Path for His Successor to declare the Nature of the whole Universe in its Form and in its Structure, as it were an Analysis thereof, doing for Matter what the Buddha was decreed to do for Mind.

Bτ

DE QUODAM MAGO AEGYPTIORUM QUEM APPELUNT JUDAEI MOSHEH

THE FOLLOWER OF TAHUTI WAS AN Egyptian whose Name is lost; but the Jews called Him Mosheh, or Moses, and their Fabulists made Him the Leader of their legendary Exodus. Yet they preserved His Word, and it is IHVH, which thou must understand also as that secret Word which thou hast seen and heard in Thunders and Lightnings in thine Initiation to the Degree thou wottest of. But this Word is itself a Plan of the Fabrick of the Universe, and upon it hath been elaborated the Holy Qabalah, whereby we have Knowledge of the Natures of all Things soever upon every Plane of By-coming, and of their Forces and Tendencies and Operations, with the Keys to their Portals. Nor did He leave any Part of His Work unfinished, unless it be that accomplished three hundred Years ago by Sir Edward Kelly, of whom also I come, as thou knowest.

On that Egyptian Magus whom the Jews call Mosheh

Bv

De Mago Arabico Mohammed

EHOLD! IN THESE CHAPTERS HAVE I THY Father restricted myself, not speaking of any immediate Echo of a Word in the World, because, these Men being long since withdrawn into their Silence, it is Their One Word, and that Alone, that resoundeth undiminished through Time. Now Mohammed, who followeth, is darkened and confused by His nearness to our own Time, so that I say not save with Diffidence that His Word ALLH may mean this or that. But I am bold concerning His Doctrine of the Unity of God, for God is Man, and he said therefore: Man is One. And His Will was to unite all Men in One Reasonable Faith: to make possible Co-operation of all Races in Science. Yet, because He arose in the Time of the greatest possible Corruption and Darkness, when every Civilization and every Religion had fallen into Ruin, by the Malice of the great Sorcerer of Nazareth, as some say, He is still hidden in the Dust of the Simoom, and we may not perceive Him in His true Self of Glory.

Nevertheless, behold, o my Son, this Mystery. His true Word was LA ALLH that is to say: (There is) No God, and LA AL is that Mystery of Mysteries which thine own Eye pierced in thine Initiation. And of that Truth have the Illusion and Falsehood enslaved the Souls of Men, as it is written in *The Book of the Magus*.

 On the Arabian Magus Mohammed

Bφ

DE SE IPSO
ΤΩΙ ΜΕΓΑΛΩΙ ΘΗΡΙΩΝΟΙ
ΤΩΙ ΛΟΓΩΙ ΑΙΩΝΟΣ
CUJUS VERBUM EST ΘΕΛΗΜΑ

MY SON! ME SEEMETH IN CERTAIN HOURS that I am myself fallen on a Time even more fearful and fatal than did Mohammed, peace be upon Him! But I read clearly the Word of the Æon, that is ABRAHADABRA wherein is the whole Mystery of the Great Work, as thou knowest. And I have *The Book of the Law*, that was given unto me by Him thou wottest of; and it is the Interpretation of the Secret Will of Man on every Plane of his By-coming; and the Word of the Law is THELEMA. Do what thou wilt shall be the whole of the Law. Now because Love is the law, love under will, do I write this Epistle for thee, that thou mayst fulfil this inmost Will of Mankind, making them capable of Light, Life, Love and Liberty by the Acceptance of this Law. And the Hindrance thereunto is but as the Shell of its Egg to an Eaglet, a Thing foreign to itself, a Protection until the Hour strike, and then an End thereof.

On the Great Beast Himself, the Logos of the Æon, whose Word is Thelema

Bχ

MANDATUM AD FILIUM SUUM

HERE I REACH FORTH MINE HANDS against thee in the Sign of the Enterer, o Son of my Bowels, for with all my magical Might I will that thou fight manfully and labour with Diligence (with Sword and Trowel, say I) in this Work. For this is the first and last of all, that thou bid every Man do What he will, in Accord with his own true Nature. Therefore also blast thou that Lie that Man is of a fallen and evil Nature. For the Word of Sin is Restriction, the Doubt of his own Godhead, the Suppression of, which is the Blasphemy against, his own Holy Spirit. Saith not *The Book of the Law* that "It is a lie, this folly against self"? Therefore to every Man, in every Circumstance, say thou: Do what thou wilt; and teach him, if he yet waver, how to discover his true Nature, earnestly and with Ardour, even as I have striven to teach thee — yea, and more also!

Bψ

QUARE FILIUM CREAVIT UT FIAT LIBERTAS

O WHAT THOU WILT! — BE THIS OUR Slogan of Battle in every Act; for every Act is Conflict. There Victory leapeth shining before us; for who may thwart True Will, which is the Order of Nature Herself? Thou hast no Right but to do thy Will; do that, and no other shall say nay. For if that Will be true, its Fulfilment is of a Surety as Daylight following Sunrise. It is as certain as the Operation of any other Law of Nature; it is Destiny. Then, if that Will be obscured, if thou turn from it to Wills diseased or perverse, how canst thou hope? Fool! even thy Turns and Twists are in the Path to thine appointed End. But thou art not sprung of a Slave's Loins; thou standest firm and straight; thou dost thy Will; and thou art chosen, nay, for this Work wast thou begotten in a Magick Bed, that thou shouldst make Men free.

Wherefore he Begat His Son: So that there be Freedom

Bω

DE SUA DEBILITATE

ISTEN ATTENTIVELY, MY SON, WHILE I with heavy Heart make Confession to thee of mine own Frailty. Thou knowest that I made Renunciation of my Wage, taking this Body immediately after my Death, the Death of Eliphaz Levi Zahed, as Men say, that I might attain to this Great Work. It is now twenty Years, as Men count years, that I came to my first Understanding of my true Nature, and aspired to that Work. Now then at the first I made no Error. I abandoned my chosen Career; I poured out my whole Fortune without one Thought; I gave my Life up utterly to the Work without keeping back the least imaginable Thing. So then I made swift Strides along the Path. But in the Dhyanas that were granted unto me in Kandy, in the Island of Lanka, I used up my whole Charge of magical Energy; and for two Years I fell away from the Work.

Γα

DE MANU QUAE MAGUM SUSTINET

OW IT MAY BE WELL THAT SUCH PERIODS of Recuperation are Necessary to such weak Souls as mine; and so no Ill. But I fell from my Will, and sought other Ends in Life; and so the Hand came upon me, and tore away that which I desired, as thou knowest; also it is written in *The Temple of Solomon the King*. Yet consider also these two Years as a necessary Preparation for that greatest of all Events which befell me in El-Kahira, in the Land of Khem, the Choice of me as the Word of the Æon. Now then for a while I worked with my Will, though not wholly; and again the Hand reached forth and smote me. This, albeit my Slackness was but as a Boy playing Truant, not a Revolt against my Self. Wherefore, despite all, I made much Progress in short Time.

ΓΒ

DE SUO PECCATO

OW THEN, WELL SCHOOLED, I STROVE NO more against my Nature, and worked with all my Will. Thou knowest well how greatly I was rewarded. Yet in this last Initiation to the Grade of Magus, wherein three-and-seventy Days, as Men count Days, is but One Day, the Ordeal grew so fierce and intolerable that I gave back a Step. I did not utterly renounce the Work, but I swore not to continue unless mine Agony were abated. But after fifteen Days, I came to myself in a certain Ordeal, wherein I knew myself finally, that I could not do other than take up that fearful Burden that had broken my Spirit. And for those fifteen Days have I not suffered infinite Things? Was not the Tree of my Work frozen, one Branch withered, and one blasted? Look no more, o my Son, upon thy Father's Shame!

Γγ

DE SUA VICTORIA PER NOMEN BABALON

ND AFTER? THIS DAWN (FOR I HAVE toiled through the Night in my great Love and Care of thee) how is it with me? It is well. For I have found my Self; I have found my Will; the Obstacles that daunted me are seen to be but Shadows of Shadows. Grace be unto Our Lady BABALON.

Thus is it written in *The Book of the Law*: Remember all ye that existence is pure joy; that all the sorrows are but as shadows; they pass & are done; but there is that which remains.

Learn then that it is in the Contemplation of Division that Sorrow is, for Division is the Formula of Choronzon. It is therefore discreet for thee to unite each Element of Sorrow with its Opposite; in whose Triumph of Hymen is Ecstasy, until by the Apprehension of the new great Opposite the Idea is again seen as Sorrow. This then is the Issue from Sorrow; and thou mayst understand that I now also am confident in the Necessity of this my Fall to prepare the Formula of Mine Exaltation. Therefore, my Son, thus hail Me: Blessing and Worship to the Beast, the Prophet of the Lovely Star.

On His Victory through the Name BABALON

Γδ

DE ARCANO NEFANDO

MY SON, LEARN THIS CONCERNING Magick, that the Yang moveth, and thus giveth itself up Eternally; but the Yin moveth not, seeking ever to enclose or restrict, reproducing in its own Likeness what Impression soever is made thereon, yet without Surrender. Now the Tao absorbeth all without Reproduction; so then let the Yang turn thereto, and not unto the Yin. And that thou mayst understand this, I say: It is a Mystery of O.T.O. For the Sun ariseth not and entereth to strike upon the High Altar of the Minster by the Great Western Gates, but by the Rose Oriel doth he make Way and Progress in His Pageant. O my Son, the Doors of Silver are wide open, and they tempt thee with their Beauty; but by the narrow Portal of Pure Gold shalt thou come more nobly to the Sanctuary. Behold! thou knowest not how perfect is this Magick; it is the dearest-bought and holiest of our Arcana. What then is like unto my Love toward Thee, that bestoweth upon thee this Treasure of my Wisdom? My Son, neglect it not; for it is the Exorcism of Exorcisms, and the Enchantment of Enchantments.

 ❧ *On the Unutterable Secret*

ΓΕ

DE ARCANO PER QUOD SPIRITUS QUIDAM IN CORPORE RECIPIATUR

ERE NOW IS ANOTHER FORMULA OF Power, good to invoke any Being to manifest in thyself. First, invoke him by the Power of all thy Spells and Conjurations, with Mind concentrated and Will vehement, toward him, as I have written in many Books. But because thou are NEMO, thou mayst safely invoke him, no matter of what Nature, within thy Circle. Now then do thou confer on him as the Guerdon of his Obedience the Dignity of a Soul seeking Incarnation, and so proceed to consecrate thine Act by performing the Mass of the Holy Ghost. Then shall that Spirit make himself Body from those Elements; and thou partaking thereof makest thine own Body his Machinery of Manifestation. And thus mayst thou work with any Spirit soever; yet this shall serve thee most in common Life. Also, the Qualities are well defined in the Cards of the Tarot, so that thou hast a clear-cut Means of developing thy Powers according to the Need of the Time. But learn also this, to work constantly under the Guidance of thine Holy Guardian Angel, so that thy Workings be alway in Harmony and Accord with thy True Will.

On the Secret through which any Spirit is Received in the Body

ΓF

DE CLAVI KABBALISTICA HUIUS ARTIS

OW THEN TO THEE WHO ART LONG SINCE Master of High Magick, it will be easy to shew how the Mass of the Holy Ghost, sung even in Ignorance, may work many a Wonder by Virtue of the Force generated being compelled to manifest on other than its own Plane. Here then is a Theory of the Mystery of the Æon, that I, being the Logos appointed thereunto, did create an Image of my Little Universe in the Mind of the Woman of Scarlet; that is, I manifested mine whole Magical Self in her Mind. Thus then in Her, as in a Mirror, have I been able to interpret myself to myself. Thou also in thine own Way hast the Power to create such an Image; but be thou sure and alert, testing constantly the Persons in that Image by the Holy Qabalah and by the True Signs of Brotherhood. For each Person therein shall be a Part of Thy Self, made individual and perfect, able to instruct thee in thy Path. Yet often there shall be others, that are to aid thee in thy Working, or to oppose it. And in this Matter thou shalt read especially the Record of thy Father his Working with Soror Ahitha (blessed be Her Name unto the Ages!) and certain others to Boot.

ΓΖ

DE MISSA SPIRITUS SANCTI

Now at last, o my Son, may I bring thee to understand the Truth of this Formula that is hidden in the Mass of the Holy Ghost. For Horus that is Lord of the Æon is the Child crowned and conquering. The formula of Osiris was, as thou knowest, a Word of Death, that is, the Force lay long in Darkness, and by Putrefaction came to Resurrection. But we take living Things, and pour in Life and Spirit of the Nature of our own Will, so that instantly and without Corruption the Child (as it were the Word of that Will) is generated; and again immediately taketh up his Habitation among us to manifest in Force and Fire. This Mass of the Holy Ghost is then the true Formula of the Magick of the Æon, even of the Æon of Horus, blessed be He in His Name Ra-Hoor-Khuit! And thou shalt bless also the Name of our Father Merlin, Frater Superior of the O.T.O., for that by Seven Years of Apprenticeship in His School did I discover this most excellent Way of Magick. Be thou diligent, o my Son, for in this Wondrous Art is no more Toil, Sorrow, and Disappointment, as it was in the dead Æon of the Slain Gods.

Γη

DE FORMULA TOTA

ERE THEN IS THY SCHEDULE FOR ALL Operations of Magick. First: thou shalt discover thy True Will, as I have already taught thee, and that Bud thereof which is the Purpose of this Operation.

Next, formulate this Bud-Will as a Person, seeking or constructing it, and naming it, according to thine Holy Qabalah, and its infallible Rule of Truth.

Third: purify and consecrate this Person, concentrating upon him, and against all else. This Preparation shall continue in all thy daily Life. Mark well: make ready a New Child immediately after every Birth.

Fourth: make an especial and direct Invocation at thy Mass, before the Introit, formulating a visible Image of this Child, and offering the Right of Incarnation.

Fifth: perform the Mass, not omitting the Epiklesis, and let there be a Golden Wedding Ring at the Marriage of thy Lion with thine Eagle.

Sixth: at the Consumption of the Eucharist accept this Child, losing thy Consciousness in him, until he be well assimilated within thee.

Now then do this continuously, for by Repetition cometh forth both Strength and Skill, and the Effect is cumulative, if thou allow no Time for it to dissipate itself.

ΓΘ

DE HAC FORMULA CONSIDERATIONES KABBALISTICAE

EHOLD MOREOVER, MY SON, THE ŒCONomy of this Way, how it is according to the Tao, fulfilling itself wholly within thine own Sphere. And it is utterly in Tune with thine own Will on every Plane, so that every Part of thy Nature rejoiceth with every other Part, communicating Praise. Now then learn also how this Formula is that of the Word ABRAHADABRA. First, HAD is the Triangle erect upon twin Squares. Of Hadit need I not to write, for He hath hidden Himself in *The Book of the Law.* The Substance is the Father, the Instrument is the Son, and the Metaphysical Ecstasy is the Holy Ghost, whose Name is HRILIU. These are then the Sun, Mercury, and Venus, whose sacred Letters are R, B, and D. But the last of the Diverse Letters is H, which in the Tarot is The Star whose Eidolon is D; and herein is that Arcanum concerning the Tao of which I have already written. Of this will I not write more plainly. But mark this, that our Trinity is our Path inwards in the Solar System, and that H being of Our Lady NUIT Starry, is an Anchor to this Magick which else were apt to deny our Wholeness of Relation to the Outer as to the Inner. My Son, ponder these Words, and profit by them; for I have wrought cunningly to conceal or to reveal, according to thine Intelligence, o my Son!

Γι

DE QUIBUSDAM ARTIBUS MAGICIS

OW OF THOSE OPERATIONS OF MAGICK by which thou seekest to display unto some other Person the Righteousness of thy Will I make haste to instruct thee. First, if thou have a reasonable Link with him by Word or Letter, it is most natural simply to create in thyself, as I have taught, a Child or Bud-Will, and let that radiate from thee through the Channel aforesaid. But if thou have no Link, the Case is otherwise, and is not easy. Here thou mayst make Communication through others, as it were by Relays; or thou mayst act directly upon his Aura by magical Means, such as the Projection of thy Scin-Læca. But unless he be sensitive and well-attuned, thou mayst fare but ill. Yet even in this Case thou mayst attain much Skill by Practice with Intelligence. In the End it is better altogether to work wholly within thine own Universe, slowly and with firm Steps advancing from the Centre, and dealing, one by one, with those unharmonized Parts of the Not-Self which lie close to thee, and impinge upon thee. This therefore closeth the Circle of my Speech, for now I am returned to that which I spake aforetime concerning the general Method of Love, and thy Development by that Way.

ΓΚ

DE MAGNO OPERE

UT NOW GIVE EAR MOST EAGERLY, THOU Son of my Loins, for I will now discourse unto thee of thine own Attainment, without which all is but Idleness. Know first that conscious Thought is but phenomenal, the Noise of thy Machine. Now Chemistry, or Al-Chem-y meaneth the Egyptian Science, and the True Magick of Egypt hath this for its Foundation. We have in our House many Substances which act directly upon the Blood, and many Practices of Virtue similar, to simulate, compose, purify, analyse, direct, or concentrate the Thought. Confer *The Book of the Law* II:22. But this Action is subtle and of many Modes, and dependeth heavily on the Conditions of the Experiment, whereof the first is thine own Will therein. Therefore I say unto thee that this is thy Work immediate and necessary, to discover openly thy Will unto thyself, and to fortify and enkindle it by all One-Pointedness of Thought and Action, so that thou mayst direct it inwards unto its Core, that is Thy Self in Thy Name HADIT. For thereby is thy Will made white with Heat so that no Dross may cling to it. But this Work is the Great Work, and standeth alone.

Γλ

DE GRADIBUS AD MAGNUM OPUS

HIS GREAT WORK IS THE ATTAINMENT of the Knowledge and Conversation of Thine Holy Guardian Angel. In the Eighth Æthyr is the Way thereof revealed. But I say: prepare thyself most heartily and well for that Battle of Love by all means of Magick. Make thyself puissant, wise, radiant in every System, and balance thyself well in thine Universe. Then with a pure Will tempered in the thousand Furnaces of thy Trials, burn up thyself within thy Self. In the Preparation thou shalt have learned how thou mayst still all Thoughts, and reach Ecstasy of Trance in many Modes. But in these Marriages thy conscious Self is Bridegroom, and the not-Self Bride, while in this Great Work thou givest up that conscious Self as Bride to thy True Self. This Operation is then radically alien from all others. And it is hard, because it is a total Reversal of the Current of the Will, and a Transmutation of its Formula and Nature. Here, o my Son, is the One Secret of Success in this Great Work: Invoke Often.

Γμ

DE FORMULA LUNAE

HUS THEN CONCERNING OPERATIONS OF the Tao with the Yang and the Yin is there enough; for thine own Art of Beauty shall divine for thee, and devise new Heavens. But in all these is the Formula of the Serpent with the Head of the Lion, and all this Magick is wrought by the Radiance and Creative Force thereof. And this Force leapeth continually from Plane to Plane, and breaketh forth from his Bonds, so that Constraint is Labour. Now then learn that the Yin hath also a Formula of Force. And the Nature of the Yin is to be still, and to encircle or limit, and it is as a Mirror, reflecting diverse Images without Change in its own Kind. So then it seeketh never to overleap the Barriers of its Plane; for this Reason it is well to use it in Operations of a very definite and restricted Type. But although it be inert, yet is it most subject to Change; for its Number is four Score and one, which is of The Moon. And these are ALIM, the Gods elemental before H, descending in their midst, made them Creative. So then thou mayst use constantly this Formula to re-arrange Things in their own Planes; and this is a most pragmatick Consideration.

Γν

DE AQUILA SUMENDA

AKE IN THIS WORK THE EAGLE ALL undefiled and virginal for thy Sacrament. And thy Technick is the Magick of Water, so that thine Act is of Nourishment, and not of Generation. Therefore the Prime Use of this Art is to build up thine own Nature. But if thou hast Skill to control the Mood of the Eagle, then mayst thou work many an admirable Effect upon thine Environment. Thou knowest how great is the Fame of Witch-Women (old and without Man) to cause Events, although they create nothing. It is this Straitness of the Channel which giveth Force to the Stream. Beware, o my Son, lest thou cling overmuch to this Mode of Magick; for it is lesser than That Other, and if thou neglect That Other, then is thy Danger fearful and imminent, for it is the Edge of the Abyss of Choronzon, where are the lonely Towers of the Black Brothers. Also, the Formulation of the Object in the Eagle is by a Species of Intoxication, so that His Nature is of Dream or Delirium, and thus there may be Illusion. For this Cause I deem it not wholly unwise if thou use this Way of Magick chiefly as a Cordial; that is, for the Fortifying of thine own Nature.

Γξ

DE MEDICINIS SECUNDUM QUATTUOR ELEMENTA

ONCERNING THE USE OF CHYMICAL Agents, and be mindful that thou abuse them not, learn that the Sacrament itself relateth to Spirit, and the Four Elements balanced thereunder, in its Perfection. So also thy Lion himself hath a fourfold Menstruum for his Serpents. Now to Fire belong Cocaine, which fortifieth the Will, loosening him from bodily Fatigue, Morphine, which purifieth the Mind, making the Thought safe, and slow, and single, Heroin, which partaketh, as it seemeth, of the Nature of these twain aforesaid, albeit in Degree less notable than either of them, and Alcohol, which is Food, that is, Fuel, for the whole Man. To Water attribute Hashish and Mescal, for they make Images, and they open the Hidden Springs of Pleasure and of Beauty. Morphine, for its Ease, hath also part in Water. Air ruleth Ethyl Oxide, for it is as a Sword, dividing asunder every Part of thee, making easy the Way of Analysis, so that thou comest to learn thyself, of what Elements thou art compact. Lastly, of the Nature of Earth are the direct Hypnotics, which operate by Repose, and restore thy Strength by laying thee as a Child in the Arms of the Great Mother, I say rather of Her material and physiological Vicegerent.

On Chemical Agents according to the Four Elements

Γο

DE VIRTUTE EXPERIENTIAE IN HAC ARTE

OT SLEEP, NOT REST, NOT PEACE, NOT Contentment are of the Will of the Hero, but these Things he hateth, and consenteth to enjoy them only with Shame of his weak Nature. But he will analyse himself without Pity, and he will do all things soever that may free and fortify his Mind and Will. Know that the Technick of the Right Use of these Magick Poisons is subtle; and since the Nature of every Man differeth from that of his Fellow, there entereth Idiosyncrasy, and thine Experience shall be thy Master in this Art. Heed also this Word following: the Right Use of these Agents is to gain a Knowledge preliminary of thine own Powers, and of High States, so that thou goest not altogether blindly and without Aim in thy Quest, ignorant of the Keys to thine own inner Being. Also, thou must work alway for a definite End, never for Pleasure or for Relaxation, except thou wilt, as a good Knight is sworn to do. And thou being Hero and Magician art in Peril of abusing the Fiery Agents only, not those of Earth, Air, or Water; because these do really work with Thee in Purity, making thee wholly what thou wouldst be, an Engine indefatigable, a Mind clear, calm and concentrated, and a Heart fierce aglow.

On the Virtue of Experience in this Art

Γπ

DE SACRAMENTO VERO

UT IN THE SACRAMENT OF THE GNOSIS, which is of the Spirit, is there naught hurtful, for its Elements are not only Food, but a true Incarnation and Quintessence of Life, Love, and Liberty, and at its Manifestation thy Lion is consecrated by pure Light of Ecstasy. Also, as this is the strongest, so also is it the most sensitive of all Things soever, and both proper and ready to take Impress of Will, not as a Seal passively, but with true Recreation in a Microcosm thereof. And this is a God alive and puissant to create, and He is a Word of Magick wherein thou mayst read Thyself with all thine History and all thy Possibility. Also as to thine Eagle, is not this chosen by Nature Herself by Her Way of Attraction, without which Harmony Æsthetic and Magnetic thy Lion is silent, and inert, even as Achilles (before his Rage) in his Tent? Now also therefore I charge thee, o my Son, to partake constantly of this Sacrament, for it is proper to all Virtue, and as thou dost learn to use it in Perfection, thou wilt surpass all other Modes of Magick. Yea, in good sooth, no Herb or Potion is like unto this, supreme in every Case, for it is the True Stone of the Philosophers, and the Elixir and Medicine of all Things, the Universal Tincture or Menstruum of Thine Own Will.

ϛϙ

DE DISCIPULIS REGENDIS

WILL HAVE THEE TO KNOW, MOREOVER, my dear Son, the right Art of Conduct with them whom I shall give thee for Initiation. And the Rule thereof is One Rule: Do what thou wilt shall be the whole of the Law. See thou constantly to it that this be not broken; especially in the Section thereof (I dare say so) which readeth Mind Thine Own Business. This is of Application equally to all, and the most dangerous Man (or Woman, as hath occurred, or I err) is the Busy-body. Oh how ashamed are we, and moved to Indignation, seeing the Sins and Follies of our Neighbours! Of all the Occasions of this Grievance the most common is the Desire of Sex unsatisfied; and thou knowest already, even in thy young Experience, how in that Delirium the Weal of the whole Universe appeareth of no account. Do thou then wean thy Babes from that Simplicity, and instil the Sense of true Proportion. For verily this is a Way of Madness, Love, unless it be under Will. And the Cure of this Madness is not so good as its Prevention, so that thou shouldst be beforehand with these Children, shewing them the right Importance of Love, how it should be a sacred Rite, exalted above Personality, and a Fire to enlighten and serve Man, not to devour him.

96 ❧ *On Directing Disciples*

Γρ

DE QUIBUSDAM MORBIS DISCIPULORUM

ND THUS, IF ANY BABE OF THINE BE ILL at ease, look closely first whether this Love be not the Root of his Distemper. Watch also Idleness, for whoso presseth eagerly forward in Will heedeth little the Affairs of his Fellows. O my Son, if every Man doth his own Will, there is no more to say! But the Busy-body nor mindeth his own Business, nor leaveth others to mind theirs. Be thou instant therefore with such an one, to cure him by enlightening his Will, and speeding him therein. Remember also that if one speak ill of another, the Fault is first of all in himself, for we know naught but that which is within us. Did not the great Witch-Finder end by confessing that he also was a Sorcerer? We become that which obsesseth us, either through extreme Hate or extreme Love. Knowest thou not how the one is a Symbol of the other? For this Reason, since Love is the Formula of Life, we are under Bond to assimilate (in the End) that which we fear or hate. So then we shall be wise to mould all Things within ourselves in Quietness and Modulation. But above all must we use all to our own End, adapting with Adroitness even our Weakness to the Work.

Γσ

DE CULPIS DOMI PETENDIS

HEREFORE, WATCH HEEDFULLY THE Fault of another, that thou mayst correct it in thyself. For if it were not in thee, thou couldst not perceive it or understand it. Lo, in thine Ecstasy of Love, thou callest upon the Universe to bear Witness that to this End alone was it created; it is unthinkable that thou shouldst love another, and incomprehensible that any Man should grieve. Yet ere the Moon change her Quarter, thou art free of thy Lunes, and lovest another, and it may be grievest in thyself while he that amazed thee hath joined the Company of the Rejoicing. Watch then, and heed thyself; and pay no heed to thy Fellows, insofar as they impede thee not. And let this be the Rule. For every Will is pure, and every Orbit free; but Error bringeth Confusion. See therefore that none leave his Path, lest he foul that of his Brother; and remember also that with Speed cometh Ease of Control. Let each Man therefore urge briskly his Chariot in a Right Line toward the Centre; for two Radii cannot cross. And beware most of this Love, because it lieth so close to Will that Dis-ease thereof easily imparteth his Error to the whole Way of the Magician.

 On Watching for Faults in the House

Γτ

DE CORPORE UMBRA HOMINIS

ONCERNING THE ÆON, O MY SON, LEARN that the Sun and His Viceregent are in all Æons, of necessity, Father, Centre, Creator, each in His Sphere of Operation. But the Formula of the past Æon was of the Dying God, and was based upon Ignorance. For Men thought that the Sun died and was reborn, alike in the Day and in the Year; and so also was the Mystery of Man. Now already are we well assured by Science how the Death of the Sun is in Truth but the Shifting of a Shadow; and in this Æon (o my Son, I lift up my Voice and I make Prophecy!) so shall it be proven as to Death. For the Body of Man is but his Shadow; it cometh and goeth even as the Tides of Ocean; and he only is in Darkness who is hidden by that Shadow from the Light of His True Self. Now therefore understand thou the Formula of Horus, the Lion God, the Child crowned and conquering that cometh forth in Force and Fire! For thy Changes are not Phases of Thee, but of the Phantoms which thou mistakest for thy Self.

Γυ

DE SIRENIS

ONCERNING THE LOVE OF WOMEN, O MY Son, it is written in *The Book of the Law* that all is Freedom, if it be done unto Our Lady Nuit. Yet also there is this Consideration, that for every Parsifal there is a Kundry. Thou mayst eat a thousand Fruits of the Garden; but there is One Tree whose Name for thee is Poison. In every great Initiation is an Ordeal, wherein appeareth a Siren or Vampire appointed to destroy the Candidate. I have myself witnessed the Blasting of not less that ten of my own Flowers, that I tended when I was NEMO, and that although I saw the Cankerworm, and knew it, and gave urgent Warning. Now then consider deeply in thyself if I were rightly governed in this Action, according to the Tao. For We that are Magicians work without Fear or Haste, being Omnipotent in Eternity, and each Star must go his Way; and who am I that I should save this People? "Wilt thou smite me, as thou smotest the Egyptian yesterday?" Yea, although mine were the Might to save these Ten, I reached not forth mine Arm against Iniquity. I spake, and I was silent; and that which was appointed came to pass. As it is written: The Pregnant Goddess hath let down Her Burden upon the Earth.

ΓΦ

DE FEMINA QUADAM

NOWEST THOU FOR WHAT CAUSE I AM moved to write this unto Thee, my Son only-begotten, Child of Magick and of Mystery? It is that I thy Father am also in this Ordeal of Initiation at this Hour. For the Sun is nigh unto the End of the Sign of the Fishes in the Thirteenth Year of the Æon, and the New Current of High Magick leapeth forth as a Flood from the Womb of my True Lady BABALON. And a Word hath come to me by the Mouth of the Scarlet Woman, whose Name is EVE, or AHITHA, concerning the Temple of IUPPITER that is builded for me. And therein is a Woman appointed to a certain Office. Now this Woman appeared to me in a Vision when I was in the House of the Juggler by the Lake among the Mountains, the Sun being in Cancer in the Eleventh Year of the Æon, even in the Week after thy Birth. And I think this Woman to be her whom I call WESRUN. But even while with a Pure Heart I did invoke Her, there came unto me another like unto Her, so that I am confused in my Mind and bewildered. And this Other Woman stirreth my true Nature in its Depth, so that I will not call it Love. For the Voice of Love I know of old; but this Other Woman speaketh in a Tongue whereof I have no Understanding.

Γχ

DE SUA VIRTUTE

HAT THEN SHALL I DO HEREIN? FOR THE Scarlet Woman adjureth me by the Great Name of God ITHUPHALLOS that I deal with this Other Woman as with any Woman, according to my Will. But this I fear, for that she is not as any Woman, and I deem her to be the Vampire of this Ordeal. How then? Shall I fear? Said I not once long since, when I was called of Men Eliphaz Levi Zahed, that the Error of Œdipus was that he should have tamed the Sphinx, and ridden her into Thebes? Shall I not take this Vampire, if she be such, and master her, and turn her to the great End? "Am I such a Man as should flee?" Is not all Fear the Word of Failure? Shall I distrust my Destiny? Am I that am the Word of the Æon of so little avail that even the whole Powers of Choronzon can disperse me? Nay, o my Son, there is Courage of Ignorance, and Discretion of Knowledge; but beyond these is Courage of Knowledge, and by no less Virtue will I win through unto mine End. As it is written: with Courage conquering Fear will I approach Thee. *Aumgn.*

Γψ

DE ALIQUIBUS MODIS ORACULI PETENDI

Y SON, IN ALL JUDGMENT AND DECISION is great Delicacy, but most in these Matters of the Will. For thou art Advocate as well as Judge, and unless thou have well organized thy Mind thou art Bondslave of Prejudice. For this Cause it is adjuvant to thy Wisdom to call Witnesses that are not of thine own Nature, and to ask Oracles whose Interpretation is bound by Fixed Rule. This is the Use of the Book TAROT, of the Divination by Earth, or by the other Elements, or by the Book *Yî-King*, and many another Mode of Truth. Thou knowest by thine Experience that these Arts deceive Thee not, save insofar as thou deceivest thyself. So then to thee that art NEMO is no Siege Perilous at this Table, but to them that are yet below the Abyss is very notable Danger of Error. Yet must they train themselves constantly in these Modes, for Experience itself shall teach them how their Bias toward their Desires reacteth in the End against themselves, and hindereth them in the Execution of their Wills. Nevertheless, as thou well knowest, the best Mode is the Creation of an Intelligible Image by Virtue of the Mass of the Holy Ghost, declaring the True Will unto thee in Terms of thy Qabalah!

Γω

DE FRATRIBUS NIGRIS FILIIS INIQUITATIS

F THE BLACK BROTHERS, O MY SON, will I write these Things following. I have told thee already concerning Change, how it is the Law, because every Change is an Act of Love under Will. So then he that is Adept Exempt, whether in Our Holy Order or another, may not remain in the Pillar of Mercy, because it is not balanced, but is unstable. Therefore is the Choice given unto him, whether he will destroy his Temple, and give up his Life, extending it to Universal Life, or whether he will make a Fortress about that Temple, and abide therein, in the false Sphere of Daäth, which is in the Abyss. And to the Adepts of Our Holy Order this Choice is terrible, by cause that they must abandon even Him whose Knowledge and Conversation they have attained. Yet, o my Son, they have much Help of Our Order in this Æon, because the General Formula is Love, so that their Habit itself urgeth them to the Bed of Our Lady BABALON. Know then the Black Brothers by these True Signs of their Initiation of Iniquity, that they resist Change, restrict and deny Love, fear Death. *Percutiantur.*

Δα

DE VIRTUTE CHIRURGICA

KNOW THAT THE CULT OF THE SLAVE-gods is Device of those Black Brothers. All that stagnateth is thereof, and thence cometh not Stability, but Putrefaction. Endure not thou the static Standards: nay, neither in Thought nor in Action. Resist not even the Change that is the Rottenness of Choronzon, but rather speed it, so that the Elements may combine by Love under Will. *Aumgn.* Since the Black Brothers and their Cults set themselves against Change, do thou break them asunder. Yea, though of bad come worse, continue in that Way; for it is as if thou didst open an Abscess, the first Effect being noisome exceedingly, but the last Cleanness. Heed not then whoso crieth Anarchy, and Immorality, and Heresy against thee, and feareth to destroy Abuse lest worse Things come of it. For the Will of the Universe in its Wholeness is to Truth, and thou dost well to purge it from its Costiveness. For it is written that there is no Bond that can unite the divided but Love, so that only those Complexes which are in truth Simplicities, being built Cell by Cell into an Unity by Virtue of Love under Will, are worthy to endure in their Progression.

Δβ

DE OPERIBUS STELLAE MICROCOSMI QUORUM SUNT QUATTUOR MINORES

I HAVE ALREADY WRITTEN UNTO THEE, O my Son, of the Paradox of Liberty, how the Freedom of thy Will dependeth upon the Bending of all thy Forces to that one End. But now learn also how great is the Œconomy of our Magick, and this will I declare unto thee in a Figure of the Holy Qabalah, to wit, the Formula of the Tetragrammaton. Firstly, the Effect of the Operation of Yod and Hé is not Vau only, but with Vau appeareth also a new Hé, as a By-Product, and She is mysterious, being at once the Flower of the Three Others, and their Poison. Now by the Operation of Vau upon that Hé is no new Creation, but the Daughter is set upon the Throne of Her Mother, and by this is rekindled the Fire of Yod, which, consuming that Virgin, doth not add a Fifth Person, but balanceth and perfecteth all. For this Shin, that is the Holy Spirit, pervadeth these, and is immanent. Thus in Three Operations is the Pentagram formulated. But in the Figure of that Star these Operations are not indicated, for the five Lines of Force connect not according to any of them; but Five New Operations are made possible; and these are the Works proper to the perfected Man. Firstly, the Work which lieth level, the Vau with the Hé, is of the Yang and the Yin, and maketh One the Human with the Divine, as in the Attainment of the Master of the Temple. Yet this Work hath its Perversion, which is of Daäth. Thus then for these Four Works, they pertain all to the Natural Formula of the Cross and Rose.

Δγ

DE OPERIBUS STELLAE MICROCOSMI QUORUM SUNT QUATTUOR MAJORES

MY SON, BEHOLD NOW THE MYSTERY and Virtue of the Silver Star! For of these Four Works not One leadeth to the Crown, because Tetragrammaton hath His Root only in Chokmah. So therefore the Formula of the Rosy Cross availeth no more in the Highest. Now then in the Pentagram are Two Lines that invoke Spirit, though they lead not thereunto, and they are the Works of Hé with Hé, and of Yod with Vau. Of these twain the former is a Work Magical of the Nature of Musick, and it draweth down the Fire of the HIGHER by Seduction or Bewitchment. Shall I say Enchantment? Shall I say Incantation? It is Song. But Bewitchment is a Work opposite thereunto, whose Effect formulateth itself by direct Creation in the Sphere of its Purpose and Intent. But there remain yet Two of the Eight Works, namely the straight Aspiration of the Chiah or Creator in thee to the Crown, and the Surrender of the Nephesch or Animal Soul to the Possession thereof; and these be the twin geodesic Formulæ of the Final Attainment, being Archetypes of the Paths of Magick (the one) and Mysticism (the other) unto the End. From each of these Eight Works is derived a separate Mode of practical Use, each after his Kind; and it should be well for thine Instruction if thou study upon these my Words, and found upon them a System. O my Son, forget not the Arcanum of their Balance and Proportion; for herein lieth the Mystery of their Holiness.

ΔΔ

DE STELLA MACROCOSMI

HUS FAR THEN CONCERNING THE PENTAgram, how it is of the Cross, and its Virtue in the Highest; but the Hexagram is for the most Part a Detail of the Formula of the Rose and Cross. Already have I shewed unto thee how the Most Holy Trinity is the Yang; but the Spirit, and the Water (or Fluid) and the Blood, that bear Witness in the Inferior, are of the Yin. Thus the Operation of the Hexagram lieth wholly within the Order of one Plane, uniting indeed any Soul with its Image, but not transcendentally, for its Effect is Cosmos, the Vau that springeth from the Union of the Yod and the Hé. Thus is it but a Glyph of only that first Formula, not of the others. But of all these Things shalt thou thyself make Study with ardent Affection; for therein lie many Mysteries of Practical Wisdom in our Magick Art. And this is the Wonder and Beauty of this Work, that for every Man is his own Palace. Yea, this is Life, that the Secrets of Our Order are not fixed and dead, as are the Formulæ of the Outer. Know that in the many thousand Times that I have performed the Ritual of the Pentagram, or the Invocation of the Heart girt with a Serpent, or the Mass of the Phœnix or of the Holy Ghost, there has not been one time wherein I did not win new Light, or Knowledge, or Power, or Virtue, save through mine own Weakness or Error.

 On the Macrocosmic Star

Δε

DE SUA FEMINA OLUN ET DE ECSTASIA PRAETER OMNIA SUBSTANTI

Y SON, I AM ENFLAMED WITH LOVE. I burn up eagerly in the Passion that thus mightily consumeth me. Yet in myself I know not at all That which constraineth me. It is Nuit herself invisibly that embraceth me, and enkindleth my Soul in Ecstasy. There is Silence in my Soul, and the Fear round about me, as I were Syrinx in the Night of the Forest. This is a great Mystery that I endure, a Mystery too great for the mortal Part of me. For but now, when I cried out upon the Name Olun עלונ, which is the secret Name of my Lady that hath come to me — most strangely! — then was I rapt away altogether subtly yet fiercely into a Trance that hath transformed me with Attainment, yet without Trace in Mind. O my Son! there is the Transfiguration of Glory, and there is the Jewel in the Lotus-flower; yea, also is many another whereof I am Partaker. But this last Passion, that my Lady Olun hath brought unto me upon this last Day of the Winter of the Thirteenth Year of the Æon, even as I wrote these Words unto thee, is a Mystery of Mysteries beyond all these. O my Son, thou knowest well the Perils and the Profit of our Path; continue thou therein. Olun! MAPIE! BABALON! *Adsum.*

On his Woman Olun, and on the Ecstasy that Surpasses All

ΔF

DE NOMINE OLUN

OUR SEASONS, OR IT MAY BE NIGH FIVE, that are past, I thy Father was in the City called New Orleans, and being in Travail of Spirit I did invoke the God that giveth Wisdom, bearing the Word of the All-Father by his Caduceus. Then suddenly, as I began, came (as it were a Gust of Fire whirled forth against that Idea) the Wit of Mine Utter Identity, so that I ceased, crying *Mercurius Sum*. Also instantly I knew in myself that there was a Mystery therein hidden, and, translating into the Greek Tongue, I exclaimed ʽΕΡΜΗΣ ʼΕΙΜΙ, whose Numeration did I make in my Mind forthwith and it is Four Hundred and Eighteen, like unto the Word of the Æon. So by this I knew that my Work was well wrought in Truth. Thus then also was it with this my Lady; for after many Questions I obtained from the Wizard Amalantrah that Name Olun, that is One Hundred and Fifty and Six even as that of Our Lady BABALON; and then, being inspired, I wrote down her Earthname in Greek, ΜΑΡΙΕ, which is also that same most Holy Number. I will have thee to wit also that this Name (as I have learned) is in the Phœnician Tongue *whôlon*; which by Interpretation is That which is Infinite, and Space; so that all is consonant rightly with NUIT Our Lady of the Stars. Thus, o my Son, is the Word of Truth echoed throughout all Worlds; and thus have the Wise mighty Assurance in Their Way. See, o my Son, that thou work not without this Guard inflexible, lest thou err in thy Perceptions.

ΔΖ

DE VIRIS MAGNANIMIS AMORE PRAECLARISSIMIS

KNOW THAT IN THE MIND OF MAN IS much Wisdom that is hidden, being the Treasure of his Sire that he inheriteth. Thus, nigh all of his Moral Nature is unknown to him until his Puberty; that is, this Nature pertaineth not unto the Recording and Judging Apparatus of his Brain until it is put therein by the Stirring of that deeper Nature within him. Thou wilt mark also that great Men are commonly great Lovers; and this is in Part because of their general Exuberance of Energy, but in Part also because (consciously or not) they are ware of this Secret following, that every Act of Love communicateth somewhat of the Wisdom stored within him to his Percipient Mind. Yet must such Act be done rightly, according to Art; and unless such Act is of Profit alike to Mind and Body, it is an Error. This then is true Doctrine; which, if it be understanded aright of thee, shall make diamond-clear thy Path in Love, which (to them that know not this) is so obscure and perilous that I believe there is not one Man in Ten Thousand that cometh not to Misadventure therein.

Δη
DE CASTITATE

Y SON, BE FERVENT! BE FIRM! BE stable! Be quick to mark Impurity, how one Course of Ideas seeketh to infringe upon another, to quell the Virtue thereof. Gold is pure, but to drink molten Gold were Impurity to thy Body, and its Destruction. Law is a Code of the Customs of a People; if it intrude thereon to alter them, it is an Impurity of Oppression. So also Diet is to be in Accord with Digestion; Ethics were an Impurity therein. Love is an Expression of the Will of the Body; yea, and more also, of That which created the Body; and its Operation is commonly between One and One, so that the Interference of any Third Person is Impurity, and not to be endured. Nay, even the Thought of a Third Person hath by Ordinary no part in Love; so that, as thou seest constantly in thy Life, Love, being strong, taketh no heed of others, and some after-Interference bringeth Misfortune. Now then shall we therefore cast out Love, or accept Impurity therein? God forbid. And for this Cause see thou well to it that in thy Kingdom there be no Interference therewith, nor Hindrance from any. For it is perfect in itself.

ΔΘ

DE CEREMONIO EQUINOCTI

Y SON, OUR FATHER IN HEAVEN HATH passed into the Sign of the Ram. It is Spring. I have performed the Rite of Union with Him according to the Antient Manner, and I know the Word that shall rule the Semester. Also it is given unto my Spirit to write unto thee concerning the Virtue of this Rite, and many another, of Antiquity. And it is this, that our Forefathers made of these Ceremonies an Epitome Mnemonic, wherein certain Truth, or True Relation, should be communicated in a magical Manner. Now therefore by the Practice of these mayst thou awaken thy Wisdom, that it may manifest in thy Conscious Mind. And this Way is of Use even when the Ceremonies, as those of the Christians, are corrupt and deformed; but in such a Case thou shalt seek out the true antient Significance thereof. For there is That within thee which remembereth Truth, and is ready to communicate the same unto thee when thou hast Wit to evoke it from the Adytum and Sanctuary of thy Being. And this is to be done by this Repetition of the Formulæ of that Truth. Note thou further that this which I tell thee is the Defence of Formalism; and indeed thou must work upon a certain Skeleton, but clothe it with live Flesh.

ΔΙ

DE LUCE STELLARUM

T WAS THAT MOST HOLY PROPHET, THINE Uncle, called upon Earth William O'Neill, or Blake, who wrote for our Understanding these Eleven sacred Words:

> If the Sun and Moon should doubt
> They'd immediately go out.

O my Son, our Work is to shine by Force and Virtue of our own Natures without Consciousness or Consideration. Now, notwithstanding that our Radiance is constant and undimmed, it may be that Clouds gathering about us conceal our Glory from the Vision of other Stars. These Clouds are our Thoughts; not those true Thoughts which are but conscious Expressions of our Will, such as manifest in our Poesy, or our Music, or other Flower-Ray of our Light quintessential. Nay, the Cloud-Thought is born of Division and of Doubt; for all Thoughts, except they be creative Emanations, are Witnesses to Conflict within us. Our settled Relations with the Universe do not disturb our Minds, as, by Example, our automatic bodily Functions, which speak to us only in the Sign of Distress. Thus all Consideration is Demonstration of Doubt; Doubt postulateth Duality, which is the Root of Choronzon.

ΔΚ

DE CANTU

O THEN, O MY SON, HERE IS MY WISDOM, that the Voice of the Soul in its true Nature Eternal and Unchangeable, comprehending All, is Silence; and the Voice of the Soul, dynamic, in the Way of its Will, is Song. Nor is there any Form of Utterance that is not, as Song is, the Music proper to that Motion, according to the Law. Thus, as thy Cousin Arthur Machen hath rejoiced to make plain unto Men in his Book called *Hieroglyphics*, the first Quality of Art is its Ecstasy. So, to nigh all Men at one Time or other, cometh Joy of Creation, with the Belief that their Utterance is holy and beautiful, glorious with Banners. This would indeed be the Case, an we could discern their Thought from their Words; but because they have no technical Skill to express themselves, they do not enable others to reproduce or re-create the original Passion which inspired them, or even any Memory thereof. Understand then what is the Agony of the Great Soul, who hath every Key of Paradise at his Girdle, when he would open the Gate of Holiness, or of Beauty, or of any Virtue soever, to the Men of his Age!

ΔΛ

DE STULTITIA HUMANA

NOW THAT A MIND CAN APPREHEND ONLY those Things with which it is already familiar, at least in Part. Moreover, it will ever interpret according to the Distortion of its own Lenses. Thus, in a great War, all Speech soever may be understood as if it were of Reference thereunto; also, a Guilty Person, or a Melancholic, may see in every Stranger an Officer of Justice, or one of them that are banded together (him seemeth) to persecute him, as the Case may be. But consider moreover that the Mysterious is ever the Terrible, for Vulgar Minds. How then when a New Word is spoken? Either it is not heard, or it is understood awry; and it evoketh Fear, and Hate as a Reaction against Fear. Then Men take him and set him at naught, and spit upon him, and scourge him, and lead him away to crucify him; and the third Day he riseth from among the Dead, and ascendeth into Heaven, and sitteth at the right Hand of God, and cometh to judge the Quick and the Dead. This, o my Son, is the History of Everyman unto whom is given a Word.

Δμ

DE SUO PROELIO

OW THEREFORE THOU SEEST HOW MEN take the Son of Science, and burn him for a Sorcerer or a Heretic; the Poet, and cast him out as Reprobate; the Painter, as deforming Nature; the Musician, as denying Harmony; and so for every New Word. How much more, then, if the Word be of Universal Import, a Word of Revolution, and of Revelation in the Deep of the Soul? A new Star: that is for the Astronomers, and maybe setteth them by the Ears. But a new Sun! That were for all Men, and a Seed of Tumult and Upheaval in every Land. Consider in thyself, therefore, what is the Might of the Adepts, the Energy of the Sanctuary, that can endow one Man with the Word of an Æon, and bring him to the End in Victory, with his Chariot wreathed in Flowers, and his Head bound round with a Fillet of blood-honoured Laurel! My Son, thou art entered into the Battle; and the Men of our Race and of our Clan return not save in Glory.

On His Struggle

Δν

DE NECESSITATE VERBI CLAMANDI

E THAT STRIVETH AGAINST HIS OWN Nature is witless; he wotteth not his Will, darkening Counsel in himself, denying his own God, and giving place to Choronzon. So then his Work becometh Hotchpot, and he is shattered and dispersed in the Abyss. Nor is it better for him if he do this for the supposed Good of another; yea, for that other is it Evil also in the End of the Matter. For to manifest thine own Division to another, and to deceive him, is but to confirm him in Blindness or Illusion, and to hinder or to deflect him in his Way. Now to do thine own Will is to leave him free to do his own Will; but to mask thy Will is to falsify one of the Beacons by which he may steer his Ship. My Son, all Division of Soul, that begetteth Nerve-storm and Insanity, cometh from wrong Adjustment to Reality, and to Fear thereof. Wilt thou then hide Truth from thy Brother, lest he suffer? Thou dost not well, but confirmest him in Iniquity, and in Illusion, and in Infirmity of Spirit.

ΔΞ

DE MYSTERIO EUCHARISTICO UNIVERSALI

Y SON, HEED ALSO THIS WORD OF THINE Uncle William O'Neill: Everything that lives is holy. Yea, and more also, every Act is holy, being essential to the Universal Sacrament. Knowing this, thou mayst conform with that which is written in *The Book of the Law*: to make no Distinction between any one Thing and any other Thing. Learn well to apprehend this Mystery, for it is the Great Gate of the College of Understanding, whereby each and all of thy Senses become constant and perpetual Witnesses of the One Eucharist, whereunto also they are Ministers. So then to thee every Phenomenon soever is the Body of Nuit in Her Passion; for it is an Event: that is, the Marriage of some one Point of View with some One Possibility. And this State of Mind is notably an Appurtenance of thy Grade of Master of the Temple, and the Unveiling of the Arcanum of Sorrow, which is thy Work, as it is written in *Liber Magi*. Moreover, this State, assimilated in the very Marrow of thy Mind, is the first Step toward the Comprehension of the Arcanum of Change, which is the Root of the Work of a Magus of Our Holy Order. O my Son, bind this within thine Heart, for its Name is the Beatific Vision.

On the Universal Eucharistic Mystery

Δο

DE RECTO IN RECTO

OW ALSO THEN I BID THEE USE ALL filial Diligence, and attend to this same Word in the Mouth of thine Earliest Ancestor (except we adventure to invoke the Name FU-HSI) in our known Genealogy, the Most Holy, the True Man, Lao-tze, that gave His Light unto the Kingdom of Flowers. For being questioned concerning the Abode of the TAO, he gave Answer that It was in the Dung. Again, the Tathagata, the Buddha, most blessed, most perfect, and most enlightened, added his Voice, that there is no Grain of Dust which shall not attain to be Arhan. Keep therefore in just Balance the Relation of Illusion to Illusion in that Aspect of Illusion, neither confusing the Planes, nor confounding the Stars, nor denying the Laws of their Reaction, yet with Eagle's Vision beholding the One Sun of the True Nature of the Whole. Verily, this is the Truth, and unto it did also Dionysus and Tahuti and Sri Krishna set the Seal of their Witness. Cleanse therefore thine Heart, o my Son, in the Waters of the Great Sea, and enkindle it with the Fire of the Holy Ghost. For this is His Peculiar Work of Sanctification.

Δπ

DE VIRGINE BEATA

NDERSTAND THEN WELL THIS MYSTERY of Universal Godliness; for it is the Naked Beauty of the Virgin of the World. Lo! since the End is Perfection, as I have already shewn unto thee, and since also every Event is inexorably and ineluctably interwoven in the Web of that Fate, it is certain that every Phenomenon is (as thou art sworn to understand) "a particular Dealing of God with thy Soul." Yea, and more also, it is a necessary Rubric in this Ritual of Perfection. Turn not therefore away thine Eyes, for that they are too pure to behold Evil; but look upon Evil with Joy, comprehending it in the Fervour of this Light that I have enkindled in thy Mind. Learn also that every Thing soever is Evil, if thou consider it as apart, static, and in Division; and thus in a Degree must thou apprehend the Mystery of Change, for it is by Virtue of Change that this Truth of Beauty and Holiness is made steadfast in the Universe. O my Son, there is no Delight sweeter than the continuous Contemplation of this Marvel and Pageant that is ever about thee; it is the Beatitude of the Beatitudes.

On the Blessed Virgin

ΔQ

DE JOCO SUAE MOECHAE

ESIST NOT CHANGE, THEREFORE, BUT ACT constantly according to thy True Nature. For here only thou standest in Sorrow, if there be a Division conscious of itself, and hindered from its Way (whose Name is Love) unto its Dissolution. It is written in *The Book of the Law* that the Pain of Division is as nothing, and the Joy of Dissolution all. Now then here is an Art and Device of Magick that I will declare unto thee, albeit it is a Peril if thou be not fixed in that Truth, and in that Beatific Vision whereof I have written in the three Chapters foregoing. And it is this, to create by Artifice a Conflict in thyself, that thou mayst take thy Pleasure in its Resolution. Of this Play is thy sweet Stepmother, my Concubine, the Holy and Adulterous Olun, sublimely Mistress; for she invoketh in her Fancy a thousand Obstacles to Love, so that she shuddereth at a Touch, swooneth at a Kiss, and suffereth Death and Hell in the Ecstasy of her Body. And this is her Art, and it is of Nuit Our Lady, for it is a Drama or Commemoration of the whole Mystery of By-coming.

Δρ

DE PERICULO JOCORUM AMORIS

ET BE THOU HEEDFUL, O MY SON, FOR this Art is set upon a Razor's Edge. In our Blood is this Great Pox of Sin, whose Word is Restriction, as Inheritance of our Sires that served the Slave-Gods. Thou must be free in the Law of Thelema, perfectly one with thy True Self, singly and wholly bound in thy True Will, before thou durst (in Prudence) invoke the Name of Choronzon, even for thy good Sport and Phantasy. It is but to pretend, thou sayest; and that is sooth; yet thou must make Pretence so well as to deceive thyself, albeit for a Moment, else were thy Sport savourless. Then, an thou have one Point of Weakness in thee, that Thought of thine may incarnate, and destroy thee. Verily, the wise Enchanter is sure beyond Doubt of his Charm ere he toy with a fanged Cobra; and thou well knowest that this Peril of Division in Thy Self is the only one that can touch thee. For all other Evil is but Elaboration of this Theme of Choronzon. Praise therefore thy sweet Stepmother, my Concubine, the Holy and Adulterous Olun; and thine own Mother Hilarion, for in this Art was she also pre-eminent.

Δσ

De Libidine Secreta

T IS SAID AMONG MEN THAT THE WORD Hell deriveth from the Verb *helan*, to hele or conceal, in the Tongue of the Anglo-Saxons. That is, it is the Concealed Place; and this, since all things are in thine own Self, is the Unconscious. How then? Because Men were already aware how this Unconscious, or Libido, is opposed, for the most part, to the Conscious Will. In the Slave-Ages this is a Truth Universal, or well nigh to it; for in such Times are Men compelled to Uniformity by the Constraint of Necessity herself. Yea, of old it was a continual Siege of every Man, of every Clan, of every Environment; and to relax Guard was then Self-Murder, or else Treachery. So then no Man might choose his Way, until he were Hunter, Fighter, Builder; nor any Woman, but she must first be Breeder. Now in the Growth of States by Organization came, stealthily stepping, a certain Security against the grossest Perils, so that a few Men could be spared from Toil to cultivate Wisdom; and this was first provided by the Selection of a Caste Pontifical. By this Device came the Alliance of King and Priest, Strength and Cunning fortifying each the other through the Division of Labour.

Δτ

DE ORDINE CIVITATUM

O PRESENTLY, O MY SON, THIS FIRST Organization among Men, by a Procedure parallel to that of the Differentiation of Protoplasm, made the State competent to explore and to control Nature; and every Profit of this Sort released more Energy, and enlarged the Class of the Learned, until, as it is this Day, only a small Proportion of any Man's Work must needs go to the Satisfaction of the first Will essential and common, the Provision of Shelter, Food, and Protection. Verily also thou seest many Women made free to live as they will, even to the Admiration and Delight of the Sage whose Eye laugheth to contemplate Mischief. Thus the Duty of every Unit toward the Whole is diminished, and also the Necessity to conform with those narrow Laws which preserve primitive Tribes in their Struggle against Environment. Thus the State need suppress only such Heresies as directly threaten its political Stability, only such Modes of Life as work manifest and proven Hurt to others, or cause general Disorder by their Scandal. Therefore, save and except he interfere thereby with the Root Laws of Common Weal, a Man is free to develop as he will according to his True Nature.

On the Organization of Communities

Δυ

DE SCIENTIAE MODO

O THE MIND OF THE PHILOSOPHER, therefore, in the Youth of an Age, any Variation in Type must appear as a Disaster; yea, verily Intelligence itself must perforce prove its Value to the Brute in Terms of Brutishness or he distrusteth and destroyeth it. Not withstanding, as thou knowest, that Variation which is fitted to his Environment is proven the Salvation of the Species. Only, among Men, his Fellows turn ever upon the Saviour, and rend him, until those who follow him in secret, and it may be unconsciously, prove their Virtue and his Wisdom by their Survival when his Persecutors perish in their Folly. But we, being secure against all primary Enemies to the Individual or the common Weal, may, nay, we must, if we would attain the Summit for our Race, devote all spare Leisure, Wealth, and Energy to the creation of Variation from the Norm, and thus by clear Knowledge bought of Experiment and of Experience, move with Eyes well open upon our True Path. So therefore our Law of Thelema is justified also of Biology and of Social Science. It is the True Way of Nature, the Right Strategy in the War of Man with his Environment; it is the Life of his Soul.

Δφ

DE MONSTRIS

AYST THOU, O MY SON, THAT NOT THUS, but by forced Training, one cometh to Perfection? This indeed is sooth, that by artificial Selection, and well-watched Growth and Environment, one hath Dogs, Horses, Pigeons, and the like, which excel their Forebears in Strength, in Beauty, in Speed, as one will. Yet is this Work but a false Magical Artifice, temporary and of Illusion; for thy Masterpieces are but Monsters, not True Variations, and if thou leave them, they revert swiftly to their own proper and authentic Type, because that Type was made fit by Experience to its Environment. So therefore every Variation must be left free to perpetuate itself or to perish, not cherished for its Beauty, or guarded for its Appeal to thine Ideal, not cut off in thy Fear thereof. For the Proof of its Virtue lieth in the Manifestation of its Power to survive; Amen, to reproduce itself after its Kind. Nurse not the Weakness of any Man, nor swaddle and cosset him, nay, not though he were Poet or Artist, because of his Value to thy Fancy; for if thou do this, he shall increase in his Infirmity, so that even his Work, for which thou lovest him, shall be enfeebled also.

Δχ

DE INFERNO PALATIO SAPIENTIAE

OW THEN THOU SEEST THAT THIS HELL, or Concealed Place within thee, is no more a Fear or Hindrance to Men of a Free Race, but the Treasure-House of the Assimilated Wisdom of the Ages, and the Knowledge of the True Way. Thus are we Just and Wise to discover this Secret in ourselves, and conform the conscious Mind therewith. For that Mind is compact solely (until it be illuminated) of Impressions and Judgments, so that its Will is but directed by the Sum of the shallow Reactions of a most limited Experience. But thy True Will is the Wisdom of the Ages of thy Generations, the Expression of that which hath fitted thee to thine Environment. Thus thy conscious Mind is often times foolish, as when thou admirest an Ideal, and wouldst attain it, but thy True Will letteth thee, so that there is Conflict, and the Humiliation of that Mind. Here will I call to Witness the common Event of "Good Resolutions" that defy the Lightning of Destiny, being puffed up by the Wind of an Indigestible Ideal putrefying within thee. Thence cometh Colic, and presently the Poison is expelled, or else thou diest. But Resolutions of True Will are mighty against Circumstance.

Δψ

DE VITIIS VOLUNTATIS SECRETAE

EARN MOREOVER CONCERNING THIS Hell, or Hidden Wisdom, that is within thee, that it is modified, little by little, through the Experience of the Conscious Mind, which feedeth it. For that Wisdom is the Expression, or rather Symbol and Hieroglyph, of the true Adjustment of thy Being to its Environment. Now, then, that Environment being eroded by Time, this Wisdom is no more perfect, for it is not Absolute, but standeth in Relation to the Universe. So then a Part thereof may become void of use, and atrophy, as (I will instance this Case) Man's Wit of Smell; and the bodily Organ corresponding degenerateth therewith. But this is an Effect of much Time, so that in thine Hell thou art like to find Elements vain, or foolish, or contrary to thy present Weal. Yet, o my Son, this Hidden Wisdom is not thy True Will, but only the Levers (I may say so) thereof. Notwithstanding, there lieth therein a Faculty of Balance, whereby it is able to judge whether any Element in itself is presently useful and benign, or else idle and malignant. Here then is a Root of Conflict between the Conscious and the Unconscious, here is a Debate concerning the right Order of Conduct, how the Will may be accomplished.

On the Defects of the Hidden Will

Δω

DE RATIONE PRAESIDIO VOLUNTATIS

my Son, in this case is there Darkness, yet this Comfort as a Lamp therein, that there is no Error in the Will, but only Doubt as to the Means of Success, else were we as Children afeared of Night. Thus we have need of naught but to consider the Matter by Wit of Reason, and of Prudence, and of Common Sense, and of Experience, and of Science, adjusting ourselves to our Environment so far as we must, and it to ourselves so far as we may. Here is the Key of Success, and its Name is the Skill to make right Use of Circumstance. This then is the Virtue of the Mind, to be the Wazir of the Will, a true Counsellor, through Intelligence of the Universe. But, o my Son, do thou lay this Word beneath thine Heart, that the Mind hath no Will, nor Right thereto, so that Usurpation bringeth forth a fatal Conflict in thyself. For the Mind is sensitive, unstable as Air, and may be led foolishly in Leash by a stronger Mind that worketh as the cunning Tool of a Will. Therefore thy Safety and Defence is to hold thy Mind to his right Function, a faithful Minister to thine own True Will, that is King of that Star whose Name is Thy Self, by Election of Nature. Heed well this, o my Son, for thy Mind Passive is rightly a Mirror to reflect all Things clearly without Prejudice, and to remain unstained by them.

Εα

De Cursu Sapientis

HEREFORE CONSIDER THIS AGAIN IN A Figure, that thy Mind is as the Marshal of an Army, to observe the Dispositions of the Enemy, and to order his own Forces rightly, according to that Information; but he hath no Will, only Obedience to the Word of his King to outwit and to overcome the Opposite. Nor doth that King make War by his own Whim, if he be wise and true, but solely because of the Necessity of his Country, and its Nature, whereof he is but Executive Officer and Interpreter, its Voice as the Marshal is its Arm. Thus then do thou understand thyself, not giving Place to thy Mind to dispute thy Will, nor through Ignorance and Carelessness allowing the Enemy to deceive thee, nor by Fear, by Imprudence and Foolhardiness, by Hesitation and Vacillation, by Disorder and the Lack of Firm Correctness, by Failure in Elasticity or in Obstinacy, each at its Moment, suffering Defeat in the Hour of Shock. So then, o my Son, this is thy Work, to know the Word of thy Will without Error, and to make perfect every Faculty of thy Mind, in right Order and Readiness to impose that Word as Law upon the Universe. So mote it be!

Eβ

DE RATIONE QUAE SINE VOLUNTATE EST FONS MANIAE

Is it not a Marvel how he that worketh with his Will, and is in constant Touch with the Reality external, maketh his Mind to serve him? How eagerly runneth it and returneth, gathering, arranging, clarifying, classifying, organising, comparing, setting in array, with Skill and Might and Energy that faileth never! Nay, my Son, in this Way thou canst be pitiless with thy Mind, and it will not rebel against thee, or neglect thine Ordinance. But now consider him that worketh not with his Will, how his Mind is Idle, not reaching out after Reality, but debating within itself of its own Affairs, like a Democracy, introspective. Then this Mind, not reacting equably and with Elasticity to the World, is lost in its own Anarchy and Civil War, so that although it work not, it is overcome by Weakness of Division, and becometh Choronzon. And unto these Words I call to my witness the Madness of the Soul of Muscovy, in this year XIII of our Æon that is ended. Therefore behold how this our Law of Thelema, Do what thou wilt, is the first Foundation of Health, whether in the Body, or the Mind, either of a simple or a complex, Organism.

Eγ

DE VERITATE QUAM FEMINAE NON DICERE LICET

MY SON, I CHARGE THEE, HOWSOEVER thou beest provoked thereunto, tell not the Truth to any Woman. For this is that which is written: Cast not thy Pearls before Swine, lest they turn again and rend thee. Behold, in the Nature of Woman is no Truth, nor Apprehension of Truth, nor Possibility of Truth; only, if thou entrust this Jewel unto them, they forthwith use it to thy Loss and Destruction. But they are ware of thine own Love of Truth, and thy Respect thereunto; so therefore they tempt thee, flattering with their Lips, that thou betray thyself to them. And they feign falsely, with every Wile, and cast about for thy Soul, until either in Love, or in Wrath, or in some other Folly thereof, thou speak Truth, profaning thy Sanctuary. So was it ever, and herein I call to my Witness Samson of Timnath, that was lost by this Error. Now for any Woman any Lie sufficeth; and think not in thine Extremity that Truth is mighty, and shall prevail, as it doth with any Man; for with a Woman her whole Craft and Device is to persuade thee of this, so that thou utter the Secret of thy Soul, and become her Prey. But so long as thou feed her with her own Food of Falsity, thou art secure.

Eδ

DE NATURA FEMINAE

HE NATURE OF WOMAN, O MY SON, IS AS thou hast learned in Our most Holy Qabalah; and she is the Clothing in Sex of Man, the Magical Image of his Will to Love. Therefore was it said by thine Uncle Wolfgang von Goethe: *Das Ewigweibliche zieht uns hinan*. But therefore also hath she no Nature of Truth, because she is but the Eidolon of an Excitement and of a Going of thy Star, and appertaineth not unto its Essence and Stability. So then to thee she is but Matter, and to her thou art but Energy; and neither is competent to the Formula of the other. Therefore also as thy Will is itself Imperfection, as I have shewed thee aforetime, thou art not in the Way of Love except thou be drest in that Robe of thine which thou callest Woman. And thou canst not lure her to this Action proper to her by thy Truth; but thou shalt, as our Grammar sayeth, assume the Mask of the Spirit, that thou mayst evoke it by Sympathy. But thou shalt appear in thy Glory only when she is in thy Power, and bewildered utterly by Ecstasy. This is a Mystery, o my Son, and of old Time it was declared in the Fable of Scylla and Charybdis, which are the Formulæ of the Rock and of the Whirlpool. Now then meditate thou strictly upon this most worthy and most adorable Arcanum, to thy Profit and Enlightenment.

Eε

DE DUOBUS PRAEMIIS VIAE

ET IT BE A TREASURE IN THINE HEART, o my Son, this Mystery that I shall next unveil before thine Eyes, o Eagle that thou art undazzled by the Brilliance of Light, that soarest continually with virile Flight to thine August Inheritance. Behold, the Beatific Vision is of two Orders, and in the Formula of the Rosie Cross it is of the Heart and is called Beauty; but in the Formula of the Silver Star (*id est*, of the Eye within the Triangle) it is of the Mind, and is called Wonder. Otherwise spoken, the former is of Art, a sensuous and creative Perception; but the latter of Science, an intellectual and intelligible Insight. Or again, in our Holy Qabalah, the one is of Tiphareth, the other of Binah; and in pure Philosophy, this is a Contemplation of the Cosmos Causal and Dynamic, and that of its Effect in Static Presentation. Now this Rapture of Art is a Virtue or Triumph of Love in his most universal Comprehension, but the Ecstasy of Science is a continual Orgasm of Light; that is, of the Mind. Thou sayest: o my Father, how may I attain to this Fullness and Perfection? Art thou there, o my Son? It is well, and blessed be the Bed wherein thou wast begotten, and the Womb of thy sweet Mother, Hilarion my Concubine, holy and adulterous, the Scarlet Woman! Amen.

Ef

DE ECSTASIA *SAMADHI* QUO MODO AB ILLIS DIFFERT

ONFUSE NOT THOU THIS BEATIFIC VISION with the Trances called Samadhi; yet is Samadhi the Pylon of the Temple thereof. For Samadhi is the Orgasm of the Coition of the Unlike, and is commonly violent, even as the Lightning cometh of the Discharge between two Vehicles of extreme difference of Potential. But, as I shewed formerly concerning Love, how each such Discharge bringeth either Component more nigh to Equilibrium, so is it in this other Matter, and by Experience thou comest constantly to Integration of Love (or what not) within thyself, just as all Effort becometh harmonious and easy by Virtue of Practice. Rememberest thou the first time that thou wast thrown into Water, thy Fear and thy Struggles, and the Vehemence of thy Joy when first thou didst swim without Support? Then little by little all Violence dieth away, because thou art adjusted to that Condition. Therefore the Fury of thine early Victory in these Arts Magical and Sciences is but the Sign of thine own Baseness and Unworthiness, since the Contrast or Differential is so overwhelming to thee; but, becoming expert and Adept, thou art balanced in the Glory, and calm, even as the Stars.

 On the Ecstasy of Samadhi and how it Differs from others

Eζ

DE ARTE AMORIS ET DELICIARUM MYSTICI

HE PATH THEREFORE UNTO THIS BEATIFIC Vision of Beauty, o my Son, is that practice of Bhakti Yoga which is written in the book called Eight Score and Fifteen, or *Astarté*, by this mine Hand when I was in Gaul the Beloved, at Montigny that is hard by the Forest of the Blue Fountain, with Agatha my Concubine, the very Soul of Love and of Musick, that had ventured herself from beneath the Cross Austral that she might seek me, to inspire and comfort me; and this was my Reward from the Masters, and Consolation in the Years of my Sorrow. But the Way that leadeth to the other Form of this Vision of Beatitude, to wit, Science, is Gñana Yoga or Raja Yoga, of which I have written only here and there, as one who should strew great Stones upon the Earth in Disorder, by Default of building them nobly into a Pyramid. And of this do I most heartily repent me, and ask of the God Thoth that He may give me (albeit at the Eleventh Hour) Virtue and Wit, that I may compose a true Book upon these Ways of Union. Thy first Step, therefore, o my Son, is to attain unto Samadhi, and to urge thyself perpetually to Repetition of thy Success therein. For it hath been said by Philosophers of old that Practice maketh Perfect, and that Manners, being the constant Habit of Life, maketh Man.

Eη

DE PRAEMIO SUMMO VERA SAPIENTIA ET BEATITUDINE PERFECTA

NOW THEN PRESENTLY SHALL IT COME TO pass that, as by Dint of each Experience that Component thereof which is within thee is attuned to it, a slight Effort shall suffice to unite thee therewith, and this without Shock, so that thou art no longer thrown back from the Trance, as exhausted, but abidest therein, almost without Knowledge of thy State. So then at last this Samadhi shall become normal to thy common Consciousness, as it were a Point of View. Thus all Things shall appear to thee very continually as to one in his first Love, by the Vision of Beauty, and by the Vision of Science thou shalt marvel constantly with Joy unfathomable at the Mystery of the Laws whereby the Universe is upheld. This is that which is written: True Wisdom and Perfect Happiness. O my Son, it is in this Contemplation that one hath the Reward of the Path, it is by this that the Tribulations are rolled away as a Stone from thy Tomb, it is with this that thou art wholly freed from the Illusions of Distinction, being absorbed into the Body of Our Lady Nuit. May She grant to thee this Beatitude; yea, not to thee only, but to all that are.

Εθ

DE INFERNO SERVORUM

NOW, O MY SON, HAVING UNDERSTOOD THE Heaven that is within thee, according to thy Will, learn this concerning the Hell of the Slaves of the Slave-Gods, that it is a true Place of Torment. For they, restricting themselves, and being divided in Will, are indeed the Servants of Sin, and they suffer, because, not being united in Love with the whole Universe, they perceive not Beauty, but Ugliness and Deformity; and, not being united in Understanding thereof, conceive only of Darkness and Confusion, beholding Evil therein. Thus at last they come, as did the Manichæans, to find, to their Terror, a Division even in the One, not that Division which we know for the Craft of Love, but a Division of Hate. And this, multiplying itself, Conflict upon Conflict, endeth in Hotchpot, and in the Impotence and Envy of Choronzon, and in the Abominations of the Abyss. And of such the Lords are the Black Brothers, who seek by their Sorceries to confirm themselves in Division. Yet in this even is no true Evil, for Love conquereth All, and their Corruption and Disintegration is also the Victory of BABALON.

Eι

RHAPSODIA DE DOMINA NOSTRA

LESSED BE SHE, AY, BLESSED UNTO THE Ages be Our Lady BABALON, that plieth Her Scourge upon me, even upon me, ΤΟ ΜΕΓΑ ΘΗΡΙΟΝ, to compel me to Creation and to Destruction, which are One, in Birth and in Death, being Love! Blessed be She, uniting the Egg with the Serpent, and restoring Man unto his Mother the Earth! Blessed be She, that offereth Beauty and Ecstasy in the Orgasm of every Change, and that exciteth thy Wonder and thy Worship by the Contemplation of Her Mind many-wiled! Blessed be She, that hath filled Her Cup with every Drop of my Blood, so that my Life is lost wholly in the Wine of Her Rapture! Behold, how She is drunken thereon, and staggereth about the Heavens, wallowing in Joy, crying aloud the Song of uttermost Love! Is not She thy true Mother among the Stars, o my Son, and hast not thou embraced Her in the Madness of Incest and of Adultery? Yea, blessed be She, blessed be Her Name, and the Name of Her Name, unto the Ages!

 A Rhapsody to Our Lady

Eκ

RHAPSODIA DE ASTRO SUO

O MY SON, KNOWEST THOU NOT THE JOY to lie in the Wilderness and to behold the Stars, in their Majesty of Motion calm and irresistible? Hast thou thought there that thou also art a Star, free because consciously in Accord with the Law and Determination of thy Being? It was thine own True Will that bound thee in thine Orbit; therefore thou speedest on thy Path from Glory unto Glory in continual Joy. O Son, o Reward of my Work, o Harmony and Completion of my Nature, o Token of my Toil, o Witness of my Love for thy sweet Mother, the holy and adulterous Hilarion my Concubine, adorable in thine Innocence as she in her Perfection, is not this verily Intoxication of the Spirit in the Innermost, to be free absolutely and eternally, to run and to return upon the Course in the Play of Love, to fulfil Nature constantly in Light and Life? "Afloat in the æthyr, o my God, my God!" Without Support, without Constraint, wing thine own Way, o Swan, o Bliss of Brightness!

A Rhapsody to His Star

Eλ

DE HARMONIA VOLUNTATIS ET PARCARUM

HIS IS THE EVIDENT AND FINAL SOLVENT of the Knot Philosophical concerning Fate and Freewill, that it is thine own Self, omniscient and omnipotent, sublime in Eternity, that first didst order the Course of thine own Orbit, so that that which befalleth thee by Fate is indeed the necessary Effect of thine own Will. These two, then, that like Gladiators have made War in Philosophy through these many Centuries, are made One by the Love under Will which is the Law of Thelema. O my Son, there is no Doubt that resolveth not in Certainty and Rapture at the Touch of the Wand of our Law, an thou apply it with Wit. Do thou grow constantly in the Assimilation of the Law, and thou shalt be made Perfect. Behold, there is a Pageant of Triumph as each Star, free from Confusion, sweepeth free in its right Orbit; all Heaven acclaimeth thee as thou goest, transcendental in Joy and in Splendour; and thy Light is as a Beacon to them that wander afar, strayed in the Night. *Amoun.*

 On the Harmony of Will and Fate

Eμ

PARENTHESIS DE QUADAM VIRGINE

OW, O MY SON, I WILL DECLARE UNTO thee the Virtue of that Part of Love which receiveth and draweth, being the Counterpart of thine own. For behold! I am moved in myself by the Absence of the Virgin that is appointed for me. And her Eagerness of Purity doth encompass me with its soft Tenderness, and twineth about me with sweet Scent, so that my Mind is enkindled with a gentle Flame, luminous and subtle, and I write unto thee as in a Dream. For in this Enchantment of her Devotion I am caught up cunningly into Beatitude, with great Joy of the Gods that have bestrewn my Way with Flowers, ay, many Flowers and Herbs of Magick and of Holiness withal to match their Beauty. Nay, o my Son, I will cease this Epistle unto thee for awhile, that I may rest in the Pleasure of this Contemplation, for it is a Solace ineffable, and Recreation like unto Sleep among the Mountains. Yea, can I wish thee more than this, that, coming to mine Age, thou mayst find a Virgin like unto this to draw thee with her Simplicity, and her embroidered Silence?

Eν

DE CONSTANTIA AMORIS CORDI CANDIDO

HINK IT NOT STRANGE, MY SON, THAT I, praising Adultery, should praise also Constancy and delight therein. For this is to state ill thy Question. Herein is Truth, and Wisdom concerning this Matter, that so long as Love be not wholly satisfied, and equilibrated by entire Fulfilment and Exchange, Constancy is a Point of thy Concentration, and Adultery a Division in thy Will. But when thou hast attained the Summit and Perfection in any Work, of what Worth is it to continue therein? Hast thou two Stomachs, as hath a Cow, to chew the Cud of a digested Love? Yet, o my Son, this Constancy is not of Necessity a Stagnation. Nay, behold the Body of Our Lady Nuit, therein are found certain twin Suns, that revolve constantly about each other. So also it may be in Love, that two Souls, meeting, discover each in the other such Wealth and Richness of Light and Love, that in one Phase of Life (or Incarnation) or even in many, they exhaust not that Treasure. Nor will I say that such are not in their Degree and Quality thrice fortunate. But to persist in Dullness, in Satiety, and in mutual Irritation and Abhorrence, is contrary to the Way of Nature. So therefore there is no Rule in any such Case, but the Law shall give Light to every one that hath it in his Heart, and by that Wisdom let him govern himself.

 ❦ *On Constancy in Love, to a Pure Heart*

Eξ

De Mysterio Mali

OREOVER, SAY NOT THOU IN THY SYLLOgism that, since every Change soever, be it the creation of a Symphony or a Poem or the Putrefaction of a Carcass, is an Act of Love, and since we are to make no Difference between any Thing and any other Thing, therefore all Changes are equal in Respect of our Praise. For though this be a Right Conclusion in the Term of thy Comprehension as a Master of the Temple, yet it is false in the Eyes of him that hath not attained to Understanding. So therefore any Change (or Phenomenon) appeareth noble or base to the imperfect Mind, according to its Consonance and Harmony with the Will that governeth that Mind. Thus, if it be thy Will to delight in Rhythm and Œconomy of Words, the Advertisement of a Commodity may offend thee; but if thou art in need of that Merchandise, thou wilt rejoice therein. Praise then or blame aught, as seemeth good unto thee; but with this Reflexion, that thy Judgment is relative to thine own Condition, and not absolute. This also is a Point of Tolerance, whereby thou shalt avoid indeed those Things that are hateful or noxious to thee, unless thou canst (in our Mode) win them by Love, by withdrawing thine Attention from them; but thou shalt not destroy them, for that they are without Doubt the Desire of another.

On the Mystery of Evil

Eo

DE VIRTUTE TOLERANTIAE

NDERSTAND THEN HEARTILY, O MY SON, that in the Light of this my Wisdom all Things are One, being of the Body or Our Lady Nuit, proper, necessary and perfect. There is then none superfluous or harmful, and there is none honourable or dishonourable more than another. Lo! in thine own Body, the vile Intestine is of more Worth to thee than the noble Hand or the proud Eye, for thou canst lose these and live, but not that. Esteem therefore a Thing in Relation to thine own Will, preferring the Ear if thou love Musick, and the Palate if thou love Wine, but the essential Organs of Life above these. Have Respect also to the Will of thy Fellow, not hindering him in his Way save as he may overly jostle thee in thine. For by the Practice of this Tolerance thou shalt come sooner to the Understanding of this Equality of all Things in Our Lady Nuit, and so the high Attainment of Universal Love. Yet in thy partial and particular Action, as thou art a Creature of Illusion, do thou maintain the right Relation of one Thing to another; fighting if thou be a Soldier, or building if thou be a Mason. For if thou hold not fast this Discipline and Proportion, which alloweth its True Will to every Part of thy Being, the Error of one shall draw all after it into Ruin and Dispersion.

Eπ

DE FORMULA DEORUM MORIENTIUM

LAS, MY SON! THIS HATH BEEN FATAL constantly to many a Man of noble Aspiration, that these Words were hidden from his Understanding. For there is a Balance in all Things, and the Body hath Charter to fulfil his Nature, even as the Mind hath. So to repress one Function is to destroy that Proportion which is wholesome, and wherein indeed all Health and Sanity have Consistency. Verily, it is the Art of Life to develop each Organ of Body and Mind, or as I may say, each Weapon of the Will to its Perfection, neither distorting any Use, nor suffering the Will of one Part to tyrannize over that of another. And this Doctrine (be it accurséd!) that Pain and Repression are wholesome and profitable in themselves is a Lie born of Sin and of Ignorance, the false Vision of the Universe and of its Laws that is the Basis of the Averse Formula of the Slain God. It is true that on Occasion one Limb must be sacrificed to save the whole Body, as when one cutteth away an Hand that is bitten by a Viper, or as when a Man giveth his Life to save his City. But this is a right and natural Subordination of the superficial and particular to the fundamental and general Will, and moreover it is a Case extraordinary, relating to Accident or Extremity, not in any Wise a Rule of Life, or a Virtue in its Absolute Nature.

EQ

DE STULTIS MALIGNIS

Y SON, THERE ARE AFFLICTIONS MANY and Woes many, that come of the Errors of Men in respect of the Will; but there is none greater than this, the Interference of the Busy-Body. For they make Pretence to know a Man's Thought better than he doth himself, and to direct his Will with more Wisdom than he, and to make Plans for his Happiness. And of all these the worst is he that sacrificeth himself for the Weal of his Fellow. He that is so foolish as not to follow his own Will, how shall he be so wise as to pursue that of another? If mine Horse balk at a Fence, should some Varlet come behind him, and strike at his Hoofs? Nay, Son, pursue thy Path in Peace, that thy Brother beholding thee may take Courage from thy Bearing, and Comfort from his Confidence that thou wilt not hinder him by thy Superfluity of Compassion. Let me not begin to tell thee of the Mischiefs that I have seen, whose Root was in Kindness, whose Flower was in Self-Sacrifice, and whose Fruit in Catastrophe. Verily I think there should be no End thereof. Strike, rob, slay thy Neighbour, but comfort him not unless he ask it of thee; and if he ask it, be wary.

Ep

APOLOGIA PRO SUIS LITTERIS

OW THEN, SAYEST THOU, CONCERNING this my Counsel unto thee? I say Sooth, it is of my Will to bring up this my Wisdom from its Silence into my conscious Mind, that I may the more easily reflect thereon. Thou art but a Pretext for my Action, and a Focus for my Light. Nevertheless, heed these my Words, for they shall profit thee, thou being of Age responsible in Judgment, and free in the Law of Thelema. Thus thou mayst read or no, concur or no, as thou wilt. Have I not tutored thee in the Way of the Balance, or of Antithesis, shewing thee the Art of Contradiction, whereby thou dost accept no Word save as the Victor in thy Mind over its Opposites, nay more, as the Child Transcendental of a Marriage of Opposites? This Book then shall serve thee but as a Food for thy Meditation, as a Wine to excite thy Mind to Love and War. It shall be unto thee as a Chariot to carry thee whither thou wilt; for I have seen in thee Independence and Sobriety of Judgment, with that Faculty (most rare, most noble!) to examine freely, neither obsequious nor rebellious to Authority.

Eσ

LAUS LEGIS THELEMA

THIS PROPERTY OF THY MIND, MY SON, is verily of sublime Virtue; for the Vulgar are befogged, and their Judgment made null, by their emotional Reaction. They are swayed by the Eloquence of a Numscull, or overpowered by a Name, or an Office, or the Magic of a Tailor; else, it may be they, being made Fools too often, reject without Reflexion even as at first they accepted. Again, they are wont to believe the best or the worst, as Hope or Fear predominateth in them at the Moment. Thus, they lose Touch of the Blade of Reality, and it pierceth them. Then they in Delirium of their Wounds increase Delusion, fortifying themselves in Belief of those Phantasies created by their Emotions or impressed upon their Silliness, so that their Minds have no Unity, or Stability, or Discrimination, but become Hotchpot, and the Ordure of Choronzon. O my Son, against this the Law of Thelema is a Sure Fortress, for through the Quest of thy True Will the Mind is balanced about it, and confirmeth its Flight, as the Feathers upon an Arrow, so that thou hast a Touchstone of Truth, Experience holding thee to Reality, and to Proportion. Now therefore see from yet another Airt of Heaven the absolute Virtue of our Law.

Eτ

DE SPHINGE AEGYPTIORUM

T IS NOW EXPEDIENT THAT I INSTRUCT thee concerning the Four Powers of the Sphinx, the Strangler, and firstly, that this most arcane of the Mysteries of Antiquity was never at any Period the Tool of the Slave-Gods, but a Witness of Horus through the dark Æon of Osiris to His Light and Truth, His Force and Fire. Thou canst by no means interpret the Sphinx in Terms of the Formula of the Slain God. This did I comprehend even when as Eliphaz Levi Zahed I walked up and down the Earth, seeking a Reconciliation of these Antagonists, which was a Task impossible, for in that Plane they have Antipathy. (Even so may no Man form a Square Magical of Four Units.) But the Light of the New Æon revealeth this Sphinx as the True Symbol of this our Holy Art of Magick under the Law of Thelema. In Her is the Equal Development and Disposition of the Forces of Nature, each in its Balanced Strength; also Her True Name is Soul of NU, having the Digamma for Phi, and endeth in Upsilon, not in Xi, so that her Orthography is ΣϜΙΝΥ whose Numeration is Six Hundred and Three Score and Six. But therein is my Riddle of Riddles. For the Root thereof is *SF*, which signifieth the Incarnation of the Spirit; and of Kin are not only the Sun, our Father, but Sumer, where Man knew himself Man, and Soma, the Divine Potion that giveth Men Enlightenment, and Scin, Light Astral, and Scire also, by a far Travelling. But especially is this Root hidden in Sus, that is of Sow, Swine, because the Most Holy must needs take its Delight under the Omphalos of the Unclean. But this was hidden by Wisdom, in order that the Arcanum should not be profaned during the Æon of the Slain God. But now it hath been given unto me to understand the Heart of Her Mystery, wherefore, o my Son, by Right of the great Love that I bear unto thee, I will inform thee thereof.

Eυ

DE NATURA ΣFINΥ

IRSTLY, THIS SPHINX IS A SYMBOL OF the Coition of Our Lady BABALON with me THE BEAST in its Wholeness. For as I am of the Lion and the Dragon, so is She of the Man and the Bull, in our Natures, but the Converse thereof in our Offices, as thou mayst understand by the Study of the Book of *The Vision and the Voice*. It is thus a Glyph of the Satisfaction and Perfection of the Will and of the Work, the Completion of the True Man as the Reconciler of the Highest with the Lowest, so for our Convenience conventionally to distinguish them. This then is the Adept, who doth Will with solid Energy as the Bull, doth Dare with fierce Courage as the Lion, doth Know with swift Intelligence as the Man, and doth Keep Silence with soaring Subtlety as the Eagle or Dragon. Moreover, this Sphinx is an Eidolon of the Law, for the Bull is Life, the Lion is Light, the Man is Liberty, the Serpent is Love. Now then this Sphinx, being perfect in true Balance, yet taketh the Aspect of the Feminine Principle, that so she may be Partner of the Pyramid, that is the Phallus, pure Image of our Father the Sun, the Unity creative. The Signification of this Mystery is that the Adept must be whole, Himself, containing all Things in true Proportion, before He maketh Himself Bride of the One Universe Transcendental, in its most Secret Virtue. And now therefore, o my Son, comprehending this Mystery by thine Intelligence, I will write further unto thee of these Four Beasts of Power.

Eφ

DE TAURO

ONCERNING THE BULL, THIS IS THY WILL, constant and unwearied, whose Letter is Vau, which is Six, the Number of the Sun. He is therefore the Force and the Substance of thy Being; but, besides this, he is the Hierophant in the Taro, as if this were said: that thy Will leadeth thee unto the Shrine of Light. And in the Rites of Mithras the Bull is slain, and his Blood poured upon the Initiate, to endow him with that Will and that Power of Work. Also in the land of Hind is the Bull sacred to Shiva, that is God among that Folk, and is unto them the Destroyer of all Things. And this God is also the Phallus, for this Will operateth through Love, even as it is written in our Own Law. Yet again, Apis the Bull of Khem hath Khephra the Beetle upon His Tongue, which signifieth that it is by this Will, and by this Work, that the Sun cometh unto Dawn from Midnight. All these Symbols are most similar in their Nature, save as the Slaves of the Slave-Gods have read their own Formula into the Simplicity of Truth. For there is Naught so plain that Ignorance and Malice may not confuse and misinterpret it, even as the Bat is dazzled and bewildered by the Light of the Sun. See then that thou understand this Bull in Terms of the Law of this our Æon of Life.

Ex De Leone

OF THE LION, O MY SON, BE IT SAID THAT this is the Courage of thy Manhood, leaping upon all Things, and seizing them for thy Prey. His Letter is Teth, whose Implication is a Serpent, and the Number thereof Nine, whereof is Aub, the Secret Fire of Obeah. Also Nine is of Jesod, uniting Change with Stability. But in *The Book of Thoth* He is the Atu called Strength, or more truly, Lust, whose Number is ELEVEN which is Aud, the Light Odic of Magick. And therein is figured the Lion, even THE BEAST, and Our Lady BABALON astride of Him, that with her Thighs She may strangle Him. Here I would have thee to mark well how these our Symbols are cognate, and flow forth the one into the other, because each Soul partaketh in proper Measure of the Mystery of Holiness, and is Kin with his Fellow. But now let me shew how this Lion of Courage is more especially the Light in thee, as Leo is the House of the Sun that is the Father of Light. And it is thus: that thy Light, conscious of itself, is the Source and Instigator of thy Will, enforcing it to spring forth and conquer. Therefore also is his Nature strong with Hardihood and Lust of Battle, else shouldst thou fear that which is unlike thee, and avoid it, so that thy Separateness should increase upon thee. For this Cause he that is defective in Courage becometh a Black Brother, and To Dare is the Crown of all thy Virtue, the Root of the Tree of true Magick.

Eψ

ALTERA DE LEONE

O! IN THE FIRST OF THINE INITIATIONS, when First the Hoodwink was uplifted from before thine Eyes, thou wast brought unto the Throne of Horus, the Lord of the Lion, and by Him enheartened against Fear. Moreover, in Minutum Mundum, the Map of the Universe, it is the Path of the Lion that bindeth the two highest Faculties of thy Mind. Again, it is Mau, the Sun at Brightness of High Noon, that is called the Lion, very lordly, in our Holy Invocation. Sekhet our Lady is figured as a Lioness, for that She is that Lust of Nuit toward Hadit which is the Fierceness of the Night of the Stars, and their Necessity; whence also is She true Symbol of thine own Hunger of Attainment, the Passion of thy Light to dare all for its Fulfilling. It is then the Possession of this Quality which determineth thy Manhood; for without it thou art not impelled to Magick, and thy Will is but the Slave's Endurance and Patience under the Lash. For this Cause, the Bull being of Osiris, was it necessary for the Masters of the Æons to incarnate me as (more especially) a Lion, and my Word is first of all a Word of Enlightenment and of Emancipation of the Will, shewing to every Man a Spring within Himself to determine His Will, that he may do that Will, and no more another's. Arise therefore, o my Son, arm thyself, haste to the Battle!

Eω

DE VIRO

EARN NOW THAT THIS LION IS A NATURAL Quality in Man, and secret, so that he is not ware thereof, except he be Adept. Therefore is it necessary for thee also To Know, by the Head of thy Sphinx. This then is thy Liberty, that the Impulse of the Lion should become conscious by Means of the Man; for without this thou art but an Automaton. This Man moreover maketh thee to understand and to adjust thyself with thine Environment, else, being devoid of Judgment, thou goest blindly upon an Headlong Path. For every Star in his Orbit holdeth not his Way obstinately, but is sensitive to every other Star, and his true Nature is to do this. O, Son, how many are they whom I have seen persisting in a fatal Course, in Sway of the Belief that their dead Rigidity was Exercise of Will! To Know: this is what teacheth thee how best thou mayst accomplish thy Will. And the Letter of the Man is Tzaddi, whose Number is Ninety which is Maim, the Water that conformeth itself perfectly with its Vessel, that seeketh constantly its Level, that penetrateth and dissolveth Earth, that resisteth Pressure maugre its Adaptability, that being heated is of Force to drive great Engines, and being frozen breaketh the Mountains in Pieces. O my Son, seek well To Know!

Fa

DE DRACONE, QUAE EST AQUILA SERPENS SCORPIO

HREEFOLD IS THE NATURE OF LOVE: Eagle, Serpent, and Scorpion. And of these the Scorpion is he that, having no Lion of Light and of Courage within him, seemeth to himself encircled by Fire, and, driving his Sting into himself, he dieth. Such are the Black Brothers, that cry: I am I; they that deny Love, restricting it to their own Nature. But the Serpent is the Secret Nature of Man, that is Life and Death, and maketh his Way through the Generations in Silence. And the Eagle is that Might of Love which is the Key of Magick, uplifting the Body and its Appurtenance unto High Ecstasy upon his Wings. It is by Virtue thereof that the Sphinx beholdeth the Sun unwinking, and confronteth the Pyramid without Shame. Our Dragon, therefore, combining the Natures of the Eagle and the Serpent, is our Love, the Organon of our Will, by whose Virtue we perform the Work and Miracle of the One Substance, as saith thine Ancestor Hermes Trismegistus, in his Tablet of Smaragda. And this Dragon is called thy Silence, because in the Hour of his Operation that within thee which saith "I" is abolished in its Conjunction with the Beloved. For this Cause also is its Letter Nun, which in our Rota is the Trump Death; and Nun hath the Value of Fifty, the Number of the Gates of Understanding.

FB

DE QUATTUOR VIRTUTIS ΣFINX

EE NOW OUR SPHINX, WITH WHAT SUBtility and Art is She made Whole! Here is thy Light, the Lion, the Necessity of thy Nature, fortified by thy Life, the Bull, the Power of Work, and guided by thy Liberty, the Man, the Wit to adapt Action to Environment. These are three Virtues in One, necessary to all proper Motion, as I may say in a Figure, the Lust of the Archer, the propulsive Force of his Arm, and the equilibrating and directing Control of his Eye. Of these three if one fail, the Mark is not hit. But hold! is not a fourth Element essential in the Work? Yea, soothly, all were vain without the Engine, Arrow and Bow. This Engine is thy Body, possessed by thee and used by thee for thy Work, yet not Part of thee, even so as are his Weapons to this Archer in my Similitude. Thus is thy Dragon to be cherished of thy Lion, but if thou lack Energy and Endurance of thy Bull, thy Tools lie idle, and if Cunning and Intelligence, with Experience also, of thy Man, thy Shaft flieth crooked. So then, o my Son, do thou perfect thyself in these Four Powers, and that with Equity.

Fγ

DE LIBRA IN QUA QUATTUOR VIRTUTES AEQUIPOLLENT

Y GÑANA YOGA COMETH THY MAN TO Knowledge; by Karma Yoga thy Bull to Will; by Raja Yoga is thy Lion brought to his Light; and to make perfect thy Dragon, thou hast Bhakta Yoga for the Eagle therein, and Hatha Yoga for the Serpent. Yet mark thou well how all these interfuse, so that thou mayst accomplish no one of the Works separately. As to make Gold thou must have Gold (it is the Word of the Alchemists) so to become The Sphinx thou must first be a Sphinx. For Naught may grow save to the Norm of its own Nature, and in the Law of its own Law, or it is but Artifice, and endureth not. So therefore is it Folly, and a Rape wrought upon Truth, to aim at aught but the Fulfilment of thine own true Nature. Order then thy Workings in Accord with thy Knowledge of that Norm as best thou mayst, not heeding the Importunity of them that prate of the Ideal. For this Rule, this Uniformity, is proper only to a Prison, and a Man liveth by Elasticity, nor endureth Rigor save in Death. But whoso groweth bodily by a Law foreign to his own Nature, he hath a Cancer, and his whole Œconomy shall be destroyed by that small Disobedience.

On the Balance in which the Four Virtues have Equal Power

Fδ

DE PYRAMIDE

OW THEN AT LAST ART THOU MADE READY to confront the Pyramid, when thou art established as a Sphinx. For It also hath the foursquare Base of Law, and the Four Triangles of Light, Life, Love, and Liberty for its Sides, that meet in a Point of Perfection that is Hadit, poised to the Kiss of Nuit. But in this Pyramid there is no Difference of Form between the Sides, as it is in thy Sphinx, for these are wholly One, save in Direction. Thou art then an Harmony of the Four by Right of thine Attainment of Adeptship, the Crown of thy Manhood, but not an Identity, as in Godhead. Therefore may it be said from one Point of Sight that thine Achievement is but a Preparation, an Adornment of the Bride for the Temple of Hymen, and his Rite. Verily, o my Son, I deem in my Wisdom that this whole Work of thy Development to Sphinx-hood cometh before the Work of Theurgy, for the Lord descendeth not upon a Temple ill-conceived, and builded awry, nor abideth in a Shrine unworthy. Accomplish then this Task in Patience, with Assiduity, not hasting furiously after Godliness. For this is most sure, that to the Beauty of a Maiden answereth the Lust of her Lord, spontaneous, and without Effort or Appeal of her Contriving.

Fε

PROLEGOMENA DE SILENTIO

UT NOW CONCERNING SILENCE, O MY Son, I will have a further Word with thee. For thereby we mean not the Muteness of him that hath a Dumb Devil. This Silence is the Dragon of thine Unconscious Nature, not only the Ecstasy or Death of thine Ego in the Operation of its Organ, but also, in its Unity with thy Lion, the Truth of thy Self. Thus is thy Silence the Way of the Tao, and all Speech a Deviation therefrom. This Lion and Dragon are therefore of thy Self, and the Man and the Bull the Feminine Counterparts thereof, being the Grace of Our Lady BABALON that She bestoweth upon thee in thine Adultery with Her. They are then as a Vesture of Honour, and a Reward, that are won by the Intensity of thy Light and of thy Love. So properly we esteem Men by the Measure of their Intelligence and of their Strength, since they are equal in their essential Godhead, so far as concerneth the Quiddity thereof. See thou closely moreover unto it, that if thou be well favoured of Our Lady, thy Lion and thy Dragon grow in like Measure, for the Excess of the Feminine is Dead Weight. The Intellectual without Virility is a Dreamer of Follies, and the laborious Giant without Courage is a Slave.

FF

DE NATURA SILENTII NOSTRI

THE NATURE OF THIS SILENCE IS SHEWN also by the God Harpocrates, the Babe in the Lotus, who is also the Serpent and the Egg, that is, the Holy Ghost. This is the most secret of all Energies, the Seed of all Being, and therefore must He be sealed up in an Ark from the Malice of the Devourers. If then by thine Art thou canst conceal thy Self in thine own Nature, this is Silence, this, and not Nullity of Consciousness, else were a Stone more perfect in Adeptship than thou. But, abiding in thy Silence, thou art in a City of Refuge, and the Waters prevail not against the Lotus that enfoldeth thee. This Ark or Lotus is then the Womb of Our Lady BABALON, without which thou wert the Prey of Nile and of the Crocodiles that are therein. Now, o my Son, mark thou well this that I will write for thine Advertisement and Behoof, that this Silence, though it be Perfection of Delight, is but the Gestation of thy Lion, and in thy Season thou must Dare, and come forth to the Battle. Else, were not this Practice of Silence akin to the Formula of Separateness of the Black Brothers?

FϚ

DE FORMULA RECTA DRACONIS

ERILY, O MY SON, HEREIN LIETH THE Danger and the Treason of thy Scorpion. For his Nature is against himself, being the deepest Ego, that is, a Being separate from the Universe; and this is the Root of the Whole Mystery of Evil. For he hath in him the Magick Power, which if he use not, he is self-poisoned, even as any Organ of the Body that refuseth its Function. So then his Cure is in his Ally the Lion, that feareth not the Crocodiles, nor hideth himself, but leapeth eagerly forward. The Path of the Mystick hath this Pitfall; that, though he unite himself with his God, his Mode is to withdraw from that which himseemeth is not God, whereby he affirmeth and confirmeth the Demon, that is, Duality. Be thou instant therefore, o my Son, to turn from every Act of Love at the Moment of full Satisfaction, flinging the Invoked Might thereof against a new Opposite; for the Formula of every Dragon is Perpetual Motion or Change, and therefore to dwell in the Satisfaction of thy Nature is a Stagnation, and a Violation thereof, making the Duality of Conflict, which is the Falling Away to Choronzon. Unto the which be Restriction in the Name of BABALON.

Fη

DE SUA CARTA COELORUM

PRAY THEE TO MARK, O MY SON, HOW the Grace of Nature was benignant at my Nativity, to the Right Balance and Formulation of my Sphinx. For Neptune was in the Sign of the Bull, giving Strength and Stability to my Spiritual Essence. Uranus was ascending in the Lion, to fortify my Magical Will with Courage, and to turn it to the Salvation of Man. In the Waterman was Saturnus, to make mine Intelligence sober, profound, and capable of Labour. Jupiter, with Mercury His Herald, was in Scorpio, harmonizing me and my Word according to the Essence of my Nature. Then of the others, Mars was exalted in the Goat, for physical Endurance of Toil; Sol was conjoined with Venus in the Balance, for Judgment in Art and in Life, and for Equability of Temper. Lastly, the Moon was in the Sign of the Fishes, her loved Abode, for a Gift of Sensitiveness and of Glamour. What then am I? I am a transient Effect of infinite Causes, a Child of Changes. There is no I, o thou that art not thou, else were I segregated, a Stagnation, a Thing of Hate and of Fear. But ever-moving, ever-changing, there is a Star in the Body of Our Lady Nuit, whose Word is None and Two.

FΘ

DE OPERE SUO

AM NOT I. THEN, SAYEST THOU, WHY IS this Word? Know, o my Son, that this First Person is but a Common Figure of the Speech of Men, whereof the Magus may avail himself without Implication of Metaphysick. Yet in the Mystery of Illusion, which is the Instrument of the Universal Will, I will not say the Harlot of Its Pleasure, are manifested these many Stars, and amongst them that Logos of the Æon of Horus whom thou callest ΤΟ ΜΕΓΑ ΘΗΡΙΟΝ and thy Father. And this is by-come through Virtue of the Intensity of the Will to Change, through many a Serpent-Phase of Life and Death, until in the Play of the Game its Manifestation is the Utterance of this Word of the Æon, this Law of Thelema, that shall be for a Season the Formula of the Magick of the Earth. Who then should inquire of the further Destiny of that Star, or of another? It is the Play of the Game, and the Operation of its Function shall suffice it. Rid thyself therefore of this Thought of "I" apart from All, but, attaining to Consciousness of All by Our True Way, contemplate the Play of Illusion by thine Instrument of Mind and Sense, leaving it without Care to continue in its own Path of Change.

Fι

DE FRATRIBUS NIGRIS

O MY SON, KNOW THIS CONCERNING THE Black Brothers, them that exult: I am I. This is Falsity and Delusion, for the Law endureth not Exception. So then these Brethren are not Apart, as they vainly think being wrought by Error; but are peculiar Combinations of Nature in Her Variety. Rejoice then even in the Contemplation of these, for they are proper to Perfection, and Adornments of Beauty, like a Mole upon the Cheek of a Woman. Shall I then say that were it of thine own Nature, even thine, to compose so sinister a Complex, thou shouldst not strive therewith, destroying it by Love, but continue in that Way? I deny not this hastily, nor affirm; nay, shall I even utter any Hint of that which I may foresee? For it is in mine own Nature to think that in this Matter the Sum of Wisdom is Silence. But this I say, and that boldly, that thou shalt not look upon this Horror with Fear, or with Hate, but accept this as thou dost all else, as a Phenomenon of Change, that is, of Love. For in a swift Stream thou mayst behold a Twig held steady for a while by the Play of the Water, and by this Analogue thou mayst understand the Nature of this Mystery of the Path of Perfection.

FK

DE ARTE ALCHYMISTICA

ILT THOU ACQUAINT THYSELF NOW FURther at my Reproof concerning this Arcanum of Alchymia, the Art Egyptian, how to make Gold? Of a Surety this is already in thy Knowledge, if thou examine by Our Holy Qabalah, what be the Forces that are the Influx upon Tiphareth, which is the Harmony and Beauty, or Sol, in every Kingdom of the Universe, so then also among Metals. Now this Influx is Fivefold. First, from the Crown descendeth the High Priestess in the Path of the Moon, for Inspiration, and Imagination, and Idea; see to it that this Virgin be Pure, for herein Error is Illusion. Next, from the Father floweth the Virtue of the Star in the Path of the Water-bearer, for Initiative, and Energy, and Determination, in the Innermost. Third, from the Mother are the Lovers in the Path of the Twins, for Intellectual Wholeness, and for Adjustment to Environment. These Three are from the Supernals, and complete the Theorick of thy Work. After this, in the Praxis and Executive thereof thou hast the Hermit as an Influence from the Sphere of Jupiter in the Path of the Virgin, for Secrecy, and for Concentration, and for Prudence. Lastly, from the Sphere of Mars, travelleth Justice in the Path of the Balance, for Good Judgment, and Tact, and Art. O my Son, in this Chapter is more Wisdom than in Ten Thousand Folios of the Alchemists! Study therefore to acquire Skill in this Method, and Experience; for this Gold is not only of the Metals, but of every Sphere, and this Key is of Virtue to enter every Palace of Perfection.

On the Alchemical Art

Fλ

DE FEMINA QUAE EST PROPRIA IOCO

O MY SON, HEAR THIS WISDOM OF EXPErience, how at thy first Sight, when I put thee into the Arms of Ahitha, thy sweet Stepmother my Concubine, such was thy Beauty that she became enamoured of thee, crying aloud: Ay me, an such be the Fruit of thy Magick, o my Master, then let me, me also, even me, give myself utterly to this Holy Art! Then did I, becoming heavy in Spirit, make Question of her, saying: To what End? and at this was she confounded and brought into Bewilderment; but after a great While, fumbling in her Ort of Mind, made Answer, like a Scarecrow in a Field, so was it for Rags and Tatters of Thought. Thus yet more atrabilious and sluggard was this Liver of thy Father, so that I fell into a Gloom nigh unto Weeping. Then she beholding me with Amazement cried upon me thus: Art thou not glad in Heart, o my Master? At this I gave a Sigh, even as one nigh unto Death. And She: if this be so, then is no Need any more for me to give myself to Magick. Thereat, perceiving yet again the Jest Universal of Our Lord Pan, was I swallowed up (like unto Jonah of the Old Fable) in the Belly of the Whale called Laughter, and it seemeth to me at this present Writing that I am like to abide therein for the Time that remaineth to me in this Body.

Fμ

DE FORMULA FEMINAE

OW THIS IS THE RIGHT POWER AND Property of a Woman, to arrange and to adjust all Things that exist in their proper Sphere, but not to create or to transcend. Therefore in all practical Matters is she of Might and of Wit to produce an Effect consonant with her Mood. And her Symbol is Water, that seeketh the Level, whether for Wrath, eating away the Mountains (yet even in this making smooth the Plains) or for Love, in Fecundity of Earth. But it is Fire of Man that hath heaved up those Mountains, in huge Turmoil. Man then maketh Mischief and Trouble by his Violence, be his Will convenient to his Environment, or antipathetic; but Woman disturbeth by Manipulation, adroit or sinister as her Mood may be of Order or of Disorder. For any Man to meddle in her Affair is Folly, for he comprehendeth not Quiet; so also for her to emulate him in his Office is Fatuity. Therefore in Magick though a Woman excel all Men in every Quality that is profitable to her for Attainment, yet she is Naught in that Work, even as a Man without Hands in the Shop of a Carpenter; for she hath not the Organism that might make Use of this Opportunity. Of all this is she aware by her Instinct, for her Nature is to Understand, even without Knowledge; and if thou doubt herein the Wisdom of thy Sire, do thou seek out a Woman (but with Precaution) and affirm these my Words. So shall she wax woundily wrath, and look grisely upon thee, proclaiming in shrill Voice her manifold Excellences, which she hath, and concern this Matter not one Whit.

FV

VERBA MAGISTRI SUI DE FEMINA

F A THOUSAND YEARS IT IS NIGH UNTO the Fiftieth Part, o my Son, since I obtained Favour in the Sight of a great Master of Truth, whom Men call Allan Bennett, so that he received me for his Discipulus in Magick. And he was instant with me in this Matter, and vehement, adjuring his Gods that this (which I have myself here above declared unto thee) was the Truth concerning the Nature of Woman. But I being but a Youth, and headstrong, and being enraptured in Love of Women, and Admiration of them, and Worship, delighting in them eagerly, and learning constantly from them, nourished by the Milk of their Mystery, as it should be for all True Men, did resist angrily the Doctrine of that Most Holy Man of God. And because (as it was written) he was a Vowed Virgin from his Birth, and had no Commerce with any in the Way of Carnality, I disabled his Judgment herein, as if he, being a Fish, had disallowed the Flight of Birds. But I, o my Son, am not wholly ignorant of Women, save as all Men must be in the Limitation of their Nature, for the Number of my Concubines is not notably or shamefully exceeded by that of the Phases of the Moon since my Birth. Many also have been my Disciples in Magick that were Women, and (more also) I do owe, acknowledging the same with open Gladness, the Greater Part of mine own Initiation and Advancement to the Operation of Women. Notwithstanding all these Things, I bow humbly before Allan Bennett, and repent mine Insolence, for his Saying was Sooth.

FΞ

DE VIA PROPRIA FEMINIS

T IS INDEED EASY FOR A WOMAN TO obtain the Experiences of Magick, in a certain Sort, as Visions, Trances, and the Like; yet they take not Hold upon her, to transform her, as with Men, but pass only as Images upon a Speculum. So then a Woman advanceth never in Magick, but remaineth the same, rightly or wrongly ordered according to the Force that moveth Her. Here therefore is the Limit of her Aspiration in Magick, to abide joyous and obedient beneath the Man that her Instinct shall divine, so that, becoming by Habit a Temple well-ordered, comely and consecrated, she may in her next Incarnation attract by her Fitness a Man-Soul. For this Cause hath Man esteemed Constancy and Patience as Qualities pre-eminent in Good Women, because by these she gaineth her Going toward our Godliness. Her Ordeal therefore is principally to resist Moods, which make Disorder, that is of Choronzon. Unto the which be Restriction in the Name of BABALON. Also, let her be content in this Way, for verily she hath a noble and an excellent Portion in our Holy Banquet, and escapeth many a Peril that is proper to us others. Only, be she in Awe and Wariness, for in her is no Principle of Resistance to Choronzon, so that if she become disordered in her Moods, as by Lust, or by Drunkenness, or by Idleness, she hath no Standard whereunto she may rally her Forces. In this see thou her Need of a well-guarded Life, and of a True Man for her God.

FO

DE HAC RE ALTERA INTELLIGENDA

MARK THEN, O MY SON, HOW IN THE Antient Books of Magick it is Man that selleth his Soul unto the Devil, but Woman that maketh Pact with him. For she hath constantly the Wit and Power to arrange Things at his Bidding, and she payeth this Price of his Alliance. But a Man hath one Jewel, and, bartering this, he becometh the Mockery of Satanas. Let then this tutor thee in thine own Art of Magick, that thou employ Women in all Practical Matters, to order them with Cunning, but Men in thy Need of Transfiguration or Transmutation. In a Trope, let the Woman direct the Chess-Play of Life, but the Man alter the Rules, if he so will. Lo! in ill Play is Mischief and Disorder, but in a New Law is Earthquake, and Destruction of the Root of Things. Therefore is Fear of any Man that is in Commerce with his Genius, for none knoweth if his Law shall amend the Game or do it Hurt; and of this the Proof is in Experience, won after the Victory of his Will, when there is no Way of Return; even thus saith the Poet, *Vestigia Nulla Retrorsum.* Nor do thou fear to create: for even as I have written in *The Book of Lies* (falsely so-called), thou canst create nothing that is not God. But beware of false Creations wrought by Women in whom is no Function thereof, for they are Phantoms, poisonous Vapours, bred of the Moon in her Witchcraft of Blood.

 Further concerning this

Fπ

DE CLAVIBUS MORTIS ET DIABOLI ARCANIS TAROT FRATERNITATIS R.C.

I T SHALL PROFIT THEE MUCH, O MY SON, or I err, that I instruct thee in the Mystery of the Paths of Nun and of Ayin, that in our Rota are figured in the Atu called Death, and in that called The Devil. Of these Nun joineth the Sun with Venus, and is referred to Scorpio in the Zodiac. This Path is perilous, for it seeketh the Level, and may abase thee, except thou take Heed unto the Going. Of its three Modes, the Scorpion destroyeth himself, as if it were a Type of Animal Pleasure. Next, the Serpent is proper to Works of Change, or Magick; yet is he poisonous also unless thou hast Wit to enchant him. Lastly, the Eagle is subtlest in this Sort, so that this Path is proper to a Transcendental Labour. Yet are all these in the Way of Death, so that thy Wand is dissolved and corroded in the Waters of the Cup, and must be renewed by Virtue of thy Nature in Her Course. For Fire is extinguished by Water; but upon Earth it burneth freely, and is inflamed by the Wind. Understand also that which is written concerning the Vesica, that it is the Mother, giving Ease, Sleep, and Death, which Consolations are eschewed by the True Man or Hero.

On the Keys of Death and The Devil, Arcana of the Tarot of the R.C. Brotherhood

FϘ

SEQUITUR DE HIS VIIS

OW THE PATH OF AYIN IS A LINK BETWEEN Mercury and the Sun, and in the Zodiac importeth the Goat. This Goat is called also Strength, and standeth in the Meridian at the Sunrise of Spring, and it is his Nature to leap upon the Mountains. So therefore is he a Symbol of true Magick, and his Name is Baphomet, wherefore did I design him as an Atu of Thoth, the Fifteenth, and put his Image in the Front of my Book, *The Ritual of High Magick*, which was the Second Part of my Thesis for the Grade of Major Adept, when I was clothed about with the Body called Alphonse Louis Constant. Now the Goat flieth not as doth the Eagle; but consider this also, that it is the true Nature of Man to dwell upon the Earth, so that his Flights are oft but Phantasy; yea, the Eagle also is bound to his Eyrie, nor feedeth upon Air. Therefore this Goat, making each Leap with Fervour, yet at all Times secure in his own Element, is a true Hieroglyph of the Magician. Mark also, this Path sheweth One continuous in Exaltation upon a Throne, and so is it the Formula of the Man, as the other was of the Woman.

FP

DE OCULO HOOR

I SAY FURTHERMORE THAT THIS PATH IS OF the Circle, and of the Eye of Horus that sleepeth not, but is vigilant. The Circle is all-perfect, equal every Way; but the Vesica hath bitter Need, and seeketh thy Medicine, that is of Right compounded for High Purpose, to ease her Infirmity. Thus is thy Will frustrated, and thy Mind distracted, and thy Work lamed, if indeed it be not brought to Naught. Also, thy Puissance in thine Art is minished, by a full Moiety, as I do esteem it. But the Eye of Horus hath no Need, and is free in his Will, not seeking a Level, not requiring a Medicine, and is fit and worthy to be the Companion and the Ally of thee in thy Work, as a Friend to thee, not Mistress and not Slave, that seek ever with Slyness and Deceit to encompass their own Ends. There is moreover a Reason in Physics for my Word; study thou this Matter in the Laws of the Changes of Nature. For Things Unlike do in their Marriage produce a Child which is relatively Stable, and resisteth Change; but Things Like increase mutually the Potential of their Particular Natures. Howbeit, each Path hath his own Use; and thou being instructed in all Ways, choose thine with Discretion.

Fσ

DE SUA INITIATIONE

MY SON, MY DELIGHT, HONEY OF THE Comb of my Life, I will say also this concerning the Odds of the Formulæ of Male and Female, that mine Initiation was ordered as followeth. First, unto the Middle of the Way, the Attainment of the Knowledge and Conversation of the Holy Guardian Angel, were these Men appointed to mine Aid, Jerome Pollitt of Kendal, Cecil Jones of Basingstoke, Allan Bennett of the Border, and Oscar Eckenstein of the Mountain, with no Woman. But after that Attainment hath Word come to me only through Women, Ouarda the Seer, and Virakam, and in mine Initiation into the Degree of Magus, the Cat 'ΙΛΑΡΙΩΝ thy Mother, Helen the Play-Actress the Serpent, with Myriamne the Drunkard and Rita the Harlot to bear Dagger and Poison; then these others Alice the Singing Woman for a Monkey, and Gerda the Madwoman for an Owl; then Catherine the Dog of Anubis, and Ahitha the Camel that renewed the Work of Virakam, with Olun the Dragon and — but here do I restrict myself in Speech, for the End is wrapped about with a Veil, as it were, the Face of a Virgin. But do thou meditate strictly upon these Things, distinguishing the right Property, Order, and Use of the one and the other in the Relative, even as thou makest them All-One, that is None, in the Absolute.

Fτ

DE HERBO SANCTISSIMO ARABICO

ECALL, O MY SON, THE FABLE OF THE Hebrews, which they brought from the City Babylon, how Nebuchadnezzar the Great King, being afflicted in his Spirit, did depart from among Men for Seven Years' Space, eating Grass as doth an Ox. Now this Ox is the Letter Aleph, and is that Atu of Thoth whose Number is Zero, and whose Name is Maat, Truth, or Maut, the Vulture, the All-Mother, being an Image of Our Lady Nuit, but also it is called the Fool, who is Parsifal, "der reine Thor," and so referreth to him that walketh in the Way of the Tao. Also, he is Harpocrates, the Child Horus, walking (as saith Daood, the Badawi that became King, in his Psalms), upon the Lion and the Dragon; that is, he is in Unity with his own Secret Nature, as I have shewn thee in my Word concerning the Sphinx. O my Son, yester Eve came the Spirit upon me that I also should eat the Grass of the Arabians, and by Virtue of the Bewitchment thereof behold that which might be appointed for the Enlightenment of mine Eyes. Now then of this may I not speak, seeing that it involveth the Mystery of the Transcending of Time, so that in One Hour of our Terrestrial Measure did I gather the Harvest of an Æon, and in Ten Lives I could not declare it.

On the Most Holy Grass of the Arabs

Fv

DE QUIBUSDAM MYSTERIIS, QUAE VIDI

ET EVEN AS A MAN MAY SET UP A MEMO-rial or Symbol to import Ten Thousand Times Ten Thousand, so may I strive to inform thine Understanding by Hieroglyph. And here shall thine own Experience serve us, because a Token of Remembrance sufficeth him that is familiar with a Matter, which to him that knoweth it not should not be made manifest, no, not in a Year of Instruction. Here first then is one amid the Uncounted Wonders of that Vision; upon a Field blacker and richer than Velvet was the Sun of all Being, alone. Then about Him were little Crosses, Greek, overrunning the Heaven. These changed from Form to Form geometrical, Marvel devouring Marvel, a Thousand Times a Thousand in their Course and Sequence, until by their Movement was the Universe churned into the Quintessence of Light. Moreover at another Time did I behold All Things as Bullæ, iridescent and luminous, self-shining in every Colour and every Combination of Colour, Myriad pursuing Myriad until by their perpetual Beauty they exhausted the Virtue of my Mind to receive them, and whelmed it, so that I was fain to withdraw myself from the Burden of that Brilliance. Yet, o my Son, the Sum of all this amounteth not to the Worth of one Dawn-Glimmer of Our True Vision of Holiness.

FΦ

DE QUODAM MODO MEDITATIONIS

NOW FOR THE CHIEF OF THAT WHICH WAS granted unto me, it was the Apprehension of those willed Changes or Transmutations of the Mind which lead into Truth, being as Ladders unto Heaven, or so I called them at that Time, seeking for a Phrase to admonish the Scribe that attended on my Words, to grave a Balustre upon the Stèle of my Working. But I make Effort in vain, o my Son, to record this Matter in Detail; for it is the Quality of this Grass to quicken the Operation of Thought it may be a Thousandfold, and moreover to figure each Step in Images complex and overpowering in Beauty, so that one hath not Time wherein to conceive, much less to utter, any Word for a Name of any one of them. Also, such was the Multiplicity of these Ladders, and their Equivalence, that the Memory holdeth no more any one of them, but only a certain Comprehension of the Method, wordless by Reason of its Subtility. Now therefore must I make by my Will a Concentration mighty and terrible of my Thought, that I may bring forth this Mystery in Expression. For this Method is of Virtue and Profit; by it mayst thou come easily and with Delight to the Perfection of Truth, it is no Odds from what Thought thou makest the first Leap in thy Meditation, so that thou mayst know how every Road endeth in Monsalvat, and the Temple of the Sangraal.

Fχ

SEQUITUR DE HAC RE

I BELIEVE GENERALLY, ON GROUND BOTH of Theory and Experience, so little as I have, that a Man must first be Initiate, and established in our Law, before he may use this Method. For in it is an Implication of our Secret Enlightenment, concerning the Universe, how its Nature is utterly Perfection. Now every Thought is a Separation, and the Medicine of that is to marry Each One with its Contradiction, as I have shewed formerly in many Writings. And thou shalt clap the one to the other with Vehemence of Spirit, swiftly as Light itself, that the Ecstasy be Spontaneous. So therefore it is expedient that thou have travelled already in this Path of Antithesis, knowing perfectly the Answer to every Glyph or Problem, and thy Mind ready therewith. For by the Property of this Grass all passeth with Speed incalculable of Wit, and an Hesitation should confound thee, breaking down thy Ladder and throwing back thy Mind to receive Impression from Environment, as at thy first Beginning. Verily, the Nature of this Method is Solution, and the Destruction of every Complexity by Explosion of Ecstasy, as every Element thereof is fulfilled by its Correlative, and is annihilated (since it loseth Separate Existence) in the Orgasm that is consummated within the Bed of thy Mind.

Fψ

SEQUITUR DE HAC RE

HOU KNOWEST RIGHT WELL, O MY SON, how a Thought is imperfect in two Dimensions, being separate from its Contradiction, but also constrained in its Scope, because by that Contradiction we do not (commonly) complete the Universe, save only that of its Discourse. Thus if we contrast Health with Sickness, we include in their Sphere of Union no more than one Quality that may be predicated of all Things. Furthermore, it is for the most Part not easy to find or to formulate the true Contradiction of any Thought as a positive Idea, but only as a Formal Negation in vague Terms, so that the ready Answer is but Antithesis. Thus to "White" one putteth not the Phrase "All that which is not White," for this is void, formless; it is neither clear, simple, nor positive in Conception; but one answereth "Black," for this hath an Image of his Significance. So then the Cohesion of Antitheticals destroyeth them only in Part, and one becometh instantly conscious of the Residue that is unsatisfied or unbalanced, whose Eidolon leapeth in thy Mind with Splendour and Joy unspeakable. Let not this deceive thee, for its Existence proveth its Imperfection, and thou must call forth its Mate, and destroy them by Love, as with the former. This Method is continuous, and proceedeth ever from the Gross to the Fine, and from the Particular to the General, dissolving all Things into the One Substance of Light.

Fω

CONCLUSIO DE HOC MODO SANCTITATIS

LEARN NOW THAT IMPRESSIONS OF SENSE have Opposites readily conceived, as long to short, or light to dark; and so with Emotions and Perceptions, as Love to Hate, or false to true; but the more Violent is the Antagonism, the more is it bound in Illusion, determined by Relation. Thus the Word "Long" hath no Meaning save it be referred to a Standard; but Love is not thus obscure, because Hate is its Twin, partaking bountifully of a Common Nature therewith. Now, hear this: it was given unto me in my Visions of the Æthyrs, when I was in the Wilderness of Sahara, by Tolga, upon the Brink of the Great Eastern Erg, that above the Abyss Contradiction is Unity, and that nothing could be true save by Virtue of the Contradiction that is contained in itself. Behold therefore, in this Method thou shalt come presently to Ideas of this Order, that include in themselves their own Contradiction, and have no Antithesis. Here then is thy Lever of Antinomy broken in thine Hand; yet, being in true Balance, thou mayst soar, passionate and eager, from Heaven to Heaven, by the Expansion of thine Idea, and its Exaltation, or Concentration as thou understandest by thy Studies in *The Book of the Law*, the Word thereof concerning Our Lady Nuit, and Hadit that is the Core of every Star. And this last Going upon thy Ladder is easy, if thou be truly Initiate, for the Momentum of thy Force in Transcendental Antithesis serveth to propel thee, and the Emancipation from the Fetters of Thought that thou hast won in that Praxis of Art maketh the Whirlpool and Gravitation of Truth of Competence to draw thee unto itself.

Zα

DE VIA SOLA SOLIS

HIS IS THE PROFIT OF MINE INTOXICATION of this holy Herb, the Grass of the Arab, that it hath shewed me this Mystery (with many others) not as a New Light, for I had that aforetime, but by its swift Synthesis and Manifestation of a long Sequence of Events in a Moment, I had Wit to analyse this Method, and to discover its Essential Law, which before had escaped the Focus of the Lens of mine Understanding. Yea, o my Son, there is no True Path of Light, save that which I have formerly made plain; yet in every Path is Profit, if thou be cunning to perceive it and to clasp it. For we win Truth oftentimes by Reflexion, or by the Composition and Selection of an Artist in his Presentation thereof, when else we were blind thereunto; lacking his Mode of Light. Yet were that Art of none avail unless we had already the Root of that Truth in our Nature, and a Bud ready to flower at the Summoning of that Sun. In Witness, nor a Boy nor a Stone hath Knowledge of the Sections of a Cone, and their Properties; but thou mayst teach these to the Boy by right Presentation, because he hath in his Nature those Laws of Mind that are consonant with our Art Mathematical, and hath Need only of Fledging (I may say this) so that he apply them consciously to the Work, when all being in Truth, that is, in the necessary Relations that rule our Illusion, he cometh in Course to Apprehension.

On the One Way of the Sun

Zβ

DE PRUDENTIA FRATERNITATIS A∴ A∴

ERE THEN, O MY SON, THAT SHALL BE mightier than all the Kings of the Earth, as it is prophesied — an thou be He! — because thou shalt establish the Law which I have given, even the Law of Thelema, here in this which I have written is a Point of Judgment in thy Work to bring into the Light of Initiation such as come unto thee, affirming their Will to this Attainment. For every One hath his own Path and his own Law, and there is no Art in Magick but to seek out that Path, and that Law, that he may pursue the one by the Right Use of the other. It shall be that one cometh unto thee, desiring Amen-Ra (I speak in a Figure or Exemplar), another Asi, a third Hoor-Pa-Kraat; or again, one seeketh Instruction in Obeah, and his Fellow in Wanga; and of all these not one in Ten Thousand shall be aware of his True Way. For albeit our Last Step is One for all, yet his Next Step is particular to each. Therefore is the Preparation of a Student that seeketh Our Holy Order of A∴ A∴ most general, informing his Mind of all known Methods, so that his Will may select among these by Instinct; then after, as a Probationer he practiseth those which he hath preferred, and by the Examination of his Record after the Period appointed thou mayst have Wisdom concerning him, to confirm him in those Ways which are thereby shewed to be germane to his True Nature.

Zγ

ALTERA DE SUA VIA

HUS I WAS BROUGHT UNTO THE KNOWLEDGE of myself in a certain Secret Grace, and as a Poet, by Jerome Pollitt of Kendal; Oscar Eckenstein of the Mountain discovered Manhood in me, teaching me to endure Hardship, and to dare many Shapes of Death; also he nurtured me in Concentration, the Art of the Mystics, but in Science without Lumber of Theology. Allan Bennett bestowed upon me the right Art of Magick, and our Holy Qabalah, with a great Treasure of Learning in many Matters, but especially concerning Egypt, and Asia, the Mysteries of their Arcane Wisdom. But of Cecil Jones had I the Great Gift of the Holy Magick of Abramelin, and he inducted me into that Order which we name not, because of the Silliness of the Profane that pretend thereto, and he brought me to the Knowledge and Conversation of the Holy Guardian Angel; also, he was the Herald of the Masters of the Temple, when They bade me Welcome to their Order, appointing a Siege for me in the City of the Pyramids, under the Night of Pan; but for Three Years I was not willing to avail myself thereof. Now mark well this, o my Son, that this Path was peculiar to the Law of my Star, and none other should follow me herein, or seek to follow me, for he hath his own proper Orbit. O my Son, err not by Generalization and Conformity, for this is of Very Idleness, and breedeth Ideals and Standards, that are Death.

More on this Path ❧

Zδ

DE PRUDENTIA ARTIS DOCENDI

EVERTHELESS, THIS ONE AFFLICTION shall touch nigh all that come to thee, and that is this Great Pox of Sin, that is our Bane inherited of the Æon of Slain Gods. Look then first of all, when any Postulant boweth before thee, whether there be not Conflict and Restriction in his Mind, and in his Will. If he deem Good and Evil to be absolute, instead of as relative to the Health of his Body, or the Weal of the Society of which he is a Member, or what not, as it may be, instruct him. Or, if he say that he will sacrifice all for Initiation, correct him, as it is written: "but whoso gives one particle of dust shall lose all in that hour." For it is Conflict if he weigh one Thing with another; and Renunciation, being sorrowful, is not worthy of Acceptance. But he must with Joy unite all he is and hath, heaping the Whole into one Billow of Love, under Will. Yea, o my Son, until thou hast brought the Postulant into our Freedom from Sin, and the Sense and Conviction thereof, he is not ready for the Path of our Magick and Illumination; because every Way soever is a Going, and this Sin is an Obstacle and a Fetter and an Hoodwink on every one of them, for it is Restriction, whether he set out by the Meditations of the Dhamma, or by our Qabalah, or by Vision, or Theurgy, or how else soever.

Ζε

DE MENTE INIMICA ANIMO

OW SHALL A MAN ATTAIN TO THE Trance where All is One, if he yet debate within his Mind concerning Virtue as a Thing Absolute? Thus, o my Son, there be those that are fuddled with Doubt whether Meat is to be eaten (I choose this as a Reference), which Habit is proper to the Lion, as Grass to the Horse, so that his right Problem is solely this, what is fitting to his own Nature. Or again, I suppose that he is in Vision, and an Angel, visiting him, imparteth a Truth contrary to his Prejudice, as it fell out in mine own Case, when I inhabited the Body of Sir Edward Kelly, or so I do in Part remember, as it seemeth albeit dimly. This nevertheless is sure (or the learned Casaubon, publishing the Record of that Word with the Magician Dee, sayeth falsely) that an Angel did declare unto Kelly the Very Axiomata of our Law of Thelema, in good Measure, and plainly; but Dee, afflicted by the Fixity of his Tenets that were of the Slave-Gods, was wroth, and by his Authority prevailed upon the other, who was indeed not wholly perfected as an Instrument, or the World ready for that Sowing. Consider also how in this very Life I was the Enemy of my own Law, and wrote down *The Book of the Law* contrary to my conscious Will by the Virtue of Obedience as a Scribe, and strove constantly to escape mine own Work, and the Utterance of my Word, until by Initiation I was made All-One.

On the Mind, Enemy of the Soul

ZF

DE ILLUMINATORUM OPERIBUS DIVERSIS

O THOU THEN UNDERSTAND HOW FEW BE they whose Work in this their present Lives is our Way of Initiation. Yet it is written in *The Book of the Law* that the Law is for all, so that thou shalt in no wise err if thou establish it as the Formula of the Æon, universal among Men. Also, even for them that are fitted to advance in our Light, there is Order and Diversity in Function, as regardeth their Work in Our Sublime Brotherhood, Thus, it might well be that, in a Profess-House of the Temple, or College of the Holy Ghost, each Knight or Brother might severally attain Experience of every Trance, unto the Perfection of all Illumination; yet by this there ought not Confusion to be confected, one usurping the appointed Office of another. For the Abbot, although he be not enlightened wholly, is yet Abbot; and the Place of the Cook, were he Saint, Arhan, and Paramahamsa in one Person, is in his Kitchen. Confound not thou in any wise therefore the Degree of Attainment of any Man with his right Function in Our Holy Order; for although by Initiation cometh the Light, and the Right, and the Might to accomplish all Works soever, yet these are inoperative save as they are able to use a Machine which is of the same Order of Things as the Effect required. As the best Swordsman hath Need of a Sword, so hath every Magician of a Body and Mind capable to the Work that he willeth; and he can do nothing, save it be proper to his Nature.

Zζ

DE EADEM RE ALTERA VERBA

Y THIS UNDERSTANDING BE THEY REbuked that make a Reproach to our Art, saying in their Insolence that if we have all Power, why are we betimes in Stress of Poverty, and in Contempt of Men, and in Pain of Disease, and so forth, mocking us, and holding our Magick for Delusion. But they behold not our Light, how it guideth us in our Path unto a Goal that is not in their Comprehension, so that we crave not that which seemeth to them the sole Food and Comfort of Life. Also, this which we attain, though it be the Essence of Omniscience and Omnipotence, informeth and moveth the Material World (so to call it) only according to the Nature of that which is therein. For the Light of the Sun (by His very Wholeness itself) sheweth a Rose red, but a Leaf green; and His Heat gathereth the Clouds, and disperseth them also. So I then, though I were perfect in Magick, might not work in Metals as a Smith, or become rich by Commerce as a Merchant; for I have not in my Nature the Engines proper to these Capacities, and therefore it is not of my Will to seek to exercise them. Here then is my Case, that I can not because I will not; and it were Conflict, should I turn thither. But let every Man become perfect in his own Work, not heeding the Rebuke of another, that some Way not his own is more Noble, or Profitable, but being constant in Mindfulness concerning his Business.

Further Words on this

Zη

DE PACE PERFECTA LUCE

HOW SHALL THEY MEASURE OUR STATURE and our Success by their Canon of Relation and Illusion, and their Ignorance of our Nature? Time is but Sequence, and a moment of Light outweigheth an Age of Darkness. What is Happiness but an Issue of the Harmony of our Consciousness with our Truth, and the Conformity of Will with Action? To the Initiate is Certainty of his Fulfilment, which to the Profane is but the Effect of Hazard, and he feareth to lose what he loveth, or thinketh he loveth. But we, loving only in Light, suffer not by Fear or by Bereavement, because to us every Event is Welcome, being right, necessary and proper to our particular Path. The Knowledge of this One Matter is the End of Dread and of Regret; make thou it the Governor of thy Mind, to rule its Pace, lest it hasten or lag by Stress of thine Environment. Now this Attainment is possible for all Mankind, since it asketh but Resolution of Complexities that already exist; so that this True Wisdom and Perfect Happiness cometh by the Acceptance of our Law, and its Use is the Key to all Locked Doors of the Soul, the Solvent of every Knot of the Mind, and the Reconcilement of every Contention. O my Son, in the Promulgation of the Law lieth the Reward of our Chief Work, the making whole of Mankind from that Conscience of Sin which divideth him, and afflicteth his Spirit.

ZΘ

DE PACE PERFECTA

O MY SON, IS IT NOT A MARVEL, THIS Light whereof we are the Quintessence and the Seed? By it are we made Whole, dissolved in the Body and in the Soul of Our Lady Nuit even as Her Lord Hadit, so that the Gnostic Sacrament of the Cosmos is perpetually Elevated before us. We behold all that is and comprehend its Mystery, and its Order in this High Mass eternally celebrated among us, acknowledging the Perfection of the Rite, neither confusing the Parts thereof, nor discriminating in Worship between them. So unto us is every Phenomenon a Shew of Godliness, proceeding continually in a Pageant that returneth unto itself, identical in the Phase of Naught as of Many, but whirling in the Orgia of Ineffable Holiness as it were a Dance that weaveth Figures of Beauty in Variety inexhaustible. Shall the Initiate bestir him, to better so prime a Perfection? Nay, this Will that was his is accomplished; he hath attained the Summit; so without Hope or Fear he abideth, and leaveth his Vehicle of Illusion and Magical Engine, that is, as Men say, his Body and Mind, to work out their Ritual of Change without his Interference. O my Son, ask not to what End! As it is written in *The Book of the Heart Girt with the Serpent*, concerning the Boy and the Swan: Is there not Joy ineffable in this aimless Winging?

Zι

De Morte

THOU HAST MADE QUESTION OF ME CONcerning Death, and this is mine Opinion, of which I say not: This is the Truth. First: in the Temple called Man is the God, his Soul, or Star, individual and eternal, but also inherent in the Body of Our Lady Nuit. Now this Soul, as an Officer in the High Mass of the Cosmos, taketh on the Vesture of his Office, that is, inhabiteth a Tabernacle of Illusion, a Body and Mind. And this Tabernacle is subject to the Law of Change, for it is complex, and diffuse, reacting to every Stimulus or Impression. If then the Mind be attached constantly to the Body, Death hath not Power to decompose it wholly, but a decaying Shell of the Dead Man, his Mind holding together for a little his Body of Light, haunteth the Earth, seeking (in its Error, that feareth Change) a new Tabernacle in some other Body. These Shells are broken away utterly from the Star that did enlighten them, and they are Vampires, obsessing them that adventure themselves into the Astral World without Magical Protection, or invoke them, as do the Spiritists. For by Death is Man released only from the Gross Body, at the first, and is complete otherwise upon the Astral Plane, as he was in his Life. But this Wholeness suffereth Stress, and its Girders are loosened, the weaker first, and after that the stronger.

Zk

De Adeptis R.C. Eschatologia

ONSIDER NOW IN THIS LIGHT WHAT shall come to the Adept, to him that hath aspired constantly and firmly to his Star, attuning the Mind unto the Musick of its Will. In him, if his Mind be knit perfectly together in itself, and conjoined with the Star, is so strong a Confection that it breaketh away easily not only from the Gross Body, but the Fine. It is this Fine Body which bindeth it to the Astral, as did the Gross to the Material, World; so then it accomplisheth willingly the Sacrament of a Second Death, and leaveth the Body of Light. But the Mind, cleaving closely by Right of its Harmony, and Might of its Love, to its Star, resisteth the Ministers of Disruption, for a Season, according to its Strength. Now, if this Star be of those that are bound by the Great Oath, incarnating without Remission because of Delight in the Cosmic Sacrament, it seeketh a new Vehicle in the Appointed Way, and indwelleth the Fœtus of a Child, and quickeneth it. And if at this Time the Mind of its Former Tabernacle yet cling to it, then is there Continuity of Character, and it may be Memory, between the two Vehicles. This, briefly and without Elaboration, is the Way of Asar in Amennti, according to mine Opinion, of which I say not: This is the Truth.

An Eschatology of the R.C. Adepts

Zλ

DE NUPTIIS SUMMIS

OW THEN TO THIS DOCTRINE, O MY SON, add thou that which thou hast learned in *The Book of the Law*, that Death is the Dissolution in the Kiss of Our Lady Nuit. This is a true Consonance as of Bass with Treble; for here is the Impulse that setteth us to Magick, the Pain of the Conscious Mind. Having then Wit to find the Cause of this Pain in the Sense of Separation, and its Cessation by the Union of Love, it is the Summit of our Holy Art to present the whole Being of our Star to Our Lady in the Nuptial of our Bodily Death. We are then to make our whole Engine the true and real Appurtenance of our Force, without Leak, or Friction, or any other Waste or Hindrance to its Action. Thou knowest well how an Horse, or even a Machine propelled by a Man's Feet, becometh as it were as Extension of the Rider, through his Skill and Custom. Thus let thy Star have profit of thy Vehicle, assimilating it, and sustaining it, so that it be healed of its Separation, and this even in Life, but most especially in Death. Also thou oughtest to increase thy Vehicle in Mass by true Growth in Balance that thou be a Bridegroom comely and well-favoured, a Man of Might, and a Warrior worthy of the Bed of so divine a Dissolution.

Ζμ

DE ARTE VOLUPTATIS DILEMMA QUAEDAM

HERE IS A NAMED OBJECTION, O MY SON, to our Thesis concerning Will that it should flow freely in its Way; *vide licet*, that for such as I am it is well, because I am endowed by Nature with a Lust insatiable in every Kind, so that the Universe itself seemeth incapable to appease it. For I have poured myself out unceasingly, in Bodily Passion, and in Battles with Men, and with Wild Beasts, and with Mountains and Deserts, and in Poetry and other Writings of the Musick of mine Imagination, and in Books of our Own Mysteries, and in Works Magical, and in Arts Plastic, and so forth, so that in mine Age I am become verily a Slave to mine own Genius; and my Law is that unless I sleep or create, my Soul is sick, and fain to claim the Reward and the Recreation of my Death. But (I hear thee say it) this is not the Case of All, or even of many, Men; but their Ort of Will is satisfied easily at its first Guerdon. Should not then their Wisdom be to resist themselves for a Space, as Water heaped up by a Dam gathereth Force, and Hunger feedeth upon Abstinence? Also, there is that which I have written in a former Chapter of the right Use of Discipline; and thirdly, this Free Flowing is without Subtility of Art, as it were an Harlot that plucketh Men by the Sleeve.

Zv

DE HOC MODO DISSOLUTIO

ERE THEREFORE WILL I WRITE DOWN the Answer to this Indictment of our Wisdom; that every Act of Will is to be made in its Perfection, which State is to be attained according to these Conditions: first, those of its own Law; second, those of its Environment. Judge thine own Case individually, each as it pleadeth; for there is no Canon or Code, since every Star hath its own Law diverse from every other. Now there is the Restraint of Conflict, which is Impotence and Disruption; but the Restraint of Discipline is a Fortification of the Will by Repose and by Preparation, as a Conqueror resteth his Armies, and feedeth them and looketh to their Furniture and to their Spirit, before he joineth the Battle. Also, there is the Restraint of Art, which includeth that other of Discipline, and its Nature is to adorn the Will and to admire its Strength and its Beauty, and to enjoy its Victory by Anticipation in full Confidence, not fearful of Time that robbeth them that are ignorant concerning him, how he is but Mirage and Illusion, incapable to besiege the Fortress of the Soul. Work thou thy Will, knowing (as I said aforetime by the Mouth of Eliphaz Levi Zahed), thyself Omnipotent, and thine Habitation Eternity. O my Son, attend well this Word, for it is an Heirloom, and a Ring of Ruby and Emerald in thine Inheritance.

 An Unravelling of this Knot

ZΞ

DE COMOEDIA QUAE PAN DICITUR

UBTLER THAN THE SERPENT OF HERMES, o my Son, is this Way of Restraint of Art, and thou shalt meet therein with the God Pan, and have him to thy Playmate. So shalt thou devise Comedy and Tragedy, as it were Settings for the Jewel of thy Will, to enhance the Beauty thereof, and to refine thy Pleasures. This is that which is written in *The Book of the Law*: "Wisdom says: be strong! Then canst thou bear more joy. Be not animal; refine thy rapture! If thou drink, drink by the eight and ninety rules of art: if thou love, exceed by delicacy; and if thou do aught joyous, let there be subtlety therein! But exceed! exceed!" Thus thou mayst even toy with thy tamed Devil of Sin, and use the Pain thereof to sharpen the Taste of thy Meat, being Adult, and thy Tongue keen to the Olive, and cloyed by the Sweet, while a Child is opposite to this in his Preference; or as a skilled Match of Love aboundeth in Pinchings, Slappings, Bitings and the like, to intensify the Bout and to prolong it. But this is Risk and Peril, unless thou be wholly Master, One in thy Will; for there is Poison in these dead Snakes, to destroy thee if thou lend them of thy Life by so little as one Doubt of thyself, as a Seed of Division.

On the Comedy which is called Pan

Zo

De Ludo Amoris

n this Mystery of the Restraint of Art is also the Secret of Illusion. Why, sayst thou, hath not Our Lady Nuit her Will of Her Lord Hadit, and He of Her, and so all ended? But this is the Play of Her Love, that She veileth Her Beauty in the Robe of Illusion many-coloured, and evadeth Him in Sport, yea, and divorceth Him from the Embrace, weaving new Modesties and Allurements in Her Dance. Now, o my Son, the full Comprehension of this Arcanum is the Fruit of Contemplation, if this be prepared by the Experience of this Art in thine own Case. But to them that understand not, and have Grief of Separation, being deceived by this Play so that they deem it the Division of Hate, She can but speak in Simplicity by that Word written in *The Book of the Law*: "To me!" For until thou love, the Play of Love is but Emptiness; and its Cruelty is cruel indeed, except thou know it to be but a Sauce to whet Appetite, and to give Emphasis of Contrast, as a Painter limneth the Light by Cunning of his Shadows. But all this Delight that thou mayst have of the Universe both in its Veils and in its Nakedness is a Reward of thine Attainment of Truth, and followeth after it. Nor canst thou comprehend this Doctrine by Mind, for the Division in thee crieth aloud in its Agony, denying it, unless thou be wholly Initiate.

Zπ

DE GAUDIO STUPRI

O MY SON, THIS SIN ITSELF THAT IS OUR Disease is but Misunderstanding of that Art of the Love of Our Lady Nuit. Yea, verily, it is all a Trick of Her Wit, and a Device of Her Delight, that Sin should appear, and also (mark thou well!) the Misapprehension of its Nature. Therefore the Pain of any Sinner in his Division and his Separation is to Her a little Spasm of Pleasure. But as for him, let him apprehend this Doctrine, and dissolve himself in Her Love. Thou then, being Initiate and Illuminated in this Truth, mayst accept thine own Sorrow, or rather that of thy Vehicle, as Lackey to the Joy that thou hast in thy True Self, the Star among the Stars of Her Body. The Adept of this our Art is not compassionate concerning Sin, in his own Vehicle or another's, unless the Healing thereof be proper to his Will, for he is aware of the whole Truth of the Matter. So goeth he upon his Way, and tighteneth not a Rein upon the Stallions of the Universe, but is content, beholding the Speed of their Course. Verily, o my Son, it is well written in *The Book of the Magus* that it is the Curse of my Grade that I must needs preach my Law unto Men. For I am afflicted in my Tabernacle on this Count, but in my Self I rejoice, and join in the Laughter of Her Love.

ZQ

DE CAECITIA PHILOSOPHORUM ANTIQUORUM

EHOLD, HOW COMFORTABLE IS THIS MY Wisdom, wherein I have resolved every Conflict soever that is or that can be, even in all Dimensions, that Antagonism of Things no less than their Limitations. I have said: Evil, be thou my Good; for it is the Magical Mirror of our Astarté, and the Caduceus of our Hermes. Now this was the Error of Elder Philosophers, that perceiving Changeful Duality as the Cause of Sorrow, they sought the Reconcilement in Unity and in Stability. But I shew thee the Universe as the Body of Our Lady Nuit, who is None and Two, with Hadit Her Lord as the Alternator of those Phases. This Universe is then a perpetual By-coming, the Vessel of every Permutation of Infinity, wherein every Phenomenon is a Sacrament, Change being the Act of Love, and Duality the Condition prodromal to that Act, even as an Axe must be taken back from a Cedar that it may deliver its Stroke. The Error therefore of these Philosophers lay in their false Assumption that Bliss, Knowledge and Being (the Qualities of their Changeless Unity) could be States. O my Son, how pitiful is their Beggary, these Paupers of Sense and of Experience and of Observation! The Emptiness of their Bellies was it that bred Phantoms of Ideal, so that they sought Joy by a Crude Denial of what Truth (or rather, Fact) they had perceived concerning the Universe, so that they set up an Idol of Death for their God, in very Rage of Hatred against the Sum of their own Selves.

 On the Blindness of the Elder Philosophers

Zp

DE HERESIA MANICHAEA

HESE PHILOSOPHERS, OR SHALL I NOT say Misosophers and Pseudo-Sophists, have been hard put to it to explain the Mystery of the Existence of their Evil. They have cried, frothing with Words, that Evil is Illusion. But if so, that Illusion is Evil; whence came it, and to what End? If their Devil created it, who created that Devil? All their Contention resolveth to this Dilemma of Change in a Changeless, Falsity in a True, Hate in a Loving, Weakness in an Almighty, Duality in a Simple, Being as they define their God. Nor do they see that they restrict their God (whom yet they would have to be All) by admitting Opposites to his Nature, even when they sum these Opposites as Illusion, since Illusion is the Denial of his Truth. But the Indians, seeing this, seek Escape by denying all Quality soever to their God, or True State, I speak of Parabrahman and of Nibbana, thus in any Reality of Thought rather denying Him or It than destroying Illusion. But in our Light we have no Need of any Denial, and accept All, yea, Illusion itself, discriminating only in our Minds between Phenomena by Comparison with some convenient Standard, for the Purpose of maintaining the Order of our Conceptions in Respect of the Relation of any Being with its Environment.

Zσ

De Veritate Rerum Mensuranda

o do thou apprehend this Wisdom, o my Son, laying it to thine Heart, as a Mistress, and hiding it in the Treasury of thy Mind as a Jewel of Enlightenment. Consider a Dream, how it is unreal in Respect of thine Experience of the Objects of thy waking Sense, but real also, both as it did in Fact impress thy Mind, and as it did express in arcane Token some Lust of thine Angel, as I have already shewed in this Letter. Consider the Play of the Chess, how its Law hath made for itself a Language and a Literature, yet it is but an arbitrary Invention, without impinging (save as it operateth though Pleasure and Interest upon Minds) on any other Sphere soever of the Universe. Equally, Things called (vulgarly) Real and Material exist in the Universe of our Consciousness only by the Apprehension of their Images in Mind through Sense; as, how is Colour Real or Material to a blind Man; or a Law mathematical true to him that is imbecile or demented. All Things therefore, even if unreal and irrational, nay, inconceivable and impossible (such as Iota in the Theorem of De Moivre), exist in one Form or another; but the Reality of any, though in itself absolute, is in Regard of its Relation with any other Thing dependent upon the Intercourse and Language between them, conscious or unconscious. Consider Azote, that hath nigh Four Parts in Five of the Air, how it is not real to direct Perception of any human Sense, but yet most real to our Lungs, diluting the Oxygen, by whose Love we were else violently combust. This is the Measure of Reality.

Zτ

DE APHORISMO UBI DICO: OMNIA SUNT

Y SON, LONG DID I AWAIT THEE, YEARNing, and with Pride and great Gladness did I bid thee Welcome to my City of the Pyramids, under the Night of Pan. Now then in my dear Love of thee will I reveal this Secret of Wisdom, which I wrote occultly in my last Chapter, in these Words: All Things Exist. Considered by Right Understanding, this is to deny that there is any Thing imaginable or unimaginable which doth not exist. That is, the Body of Our Lady Nuit hath no Limit, and there is no Void that She filleth not with the Variety and Beauty of Her Stars in Her Space. Nor is there any one Law of Her Nature, but in Her are all Laws, so that each Thing or each Truth that thou perceiveth is as it were one Gesture of Her Dance. Shut up the Book of thy Questions, o my Son, concerning Nature, her Way, her Origin, or her Purpose, except in those Matters which concern thee and thine own Orbit, o thou Star, begotten of my Loins in my Lust of Hilarion, the Golden Rose, mystic and joyous, the Lily of a Thousand Petals and One Petal, subtle and perverse, that thou mightest fulfil this Work of a Magus which I came to accomplish, robing myself in Flesh of Man, as was my Nature and the Will of my Nature, the Name of my Star that flameth in the Body of Nuit Our Lady.

Zv

DE RATIONE HUIUS EPISTOLAE SCRIBENDAE

BEHOLD, I DRAW UNTO THE END OF THIS Discourse of Wisdom, as a Ship that hath adventured upon Ocean, from whose Mast the Watcher espieth in the Dimness of the Horizon a Point of Snow, being the Peak of a Great Mountain that is Guardian of the Harbour, the Term of that Voyage. So now do I commit thee wholly unto thyself, for I exist not in thine Universe save in my Relation with thee; wherefore that Part of me is in Truth thou rather than I. Yet do thou treasure this Letter, for it is mine Especial Gift, and hath Radiance of the Light of my Wisdom, and flameth, being the Blood of my Love of thee and of Mankind. Also, it is as the Pulse of my Life, beating with the Nature thereof; and it is the Word of my Will, the Charter of the Liberty of my Soul, and thine, and that of every Man, and every Woman; for we are Stars. O my Son, for many Days was I silent, until thou wast fearful lest thou hadst, in Ignorance or by Inadvertence, enkindled the Fire of my Wrath. But I spake not, because I knew in my Wisdom that thou must pass a certain Ordeal of thine Initiation by thine own Virtue. For this Cause I held aloof; but in my Love I made a Beginning of this Letter, beholding thy Triumph aforehand, and with Prescience, divining thy next Need, that is to say, this Book of the Words of my Wisdom.

Zφ

DE NATURA HUIUS EPISTOLAE

MY SON, IN THIS LETTER HAVE I WRITten the Name of my own Nature, its Law, its Quality, its Will and its Appurtenance or Ornament. For it is the Child of my Love toward thee, and the Expression through mine Art of my Will so far as that regardeth thee. Now every Child is made of the Essence of his Father, so that every Creation is a Likeness or Image of the Creator, but modified by the Mother, that is to say, the Material whereon he begetteth it. So then this Letter is a Projection of mine own Star in a Mirror, to wit, mine Idea in thy Regard; and it shall be unto thee as a clear Vision of thy Father, and of the Word of the Æon that he hath uttered unto Man. But also, because this Word is the Formula of the Æon, that is to say the Law of its Changes or Phenomena, the Equation that expresseth its Energy and its Motion, it shall serve every Man in his Measure as a Text-Book or Comment upon the Theorick and Praxis of Magick. By it may he discover his own Nature, and its Will, and apply his Force and his Intelligence to the Right Fulfilment thereof. It shall be a Beacon to enlighten him, to comfort him, and to direct him; and it shall be a Witness and Memorial of my Word and of my Work, as of mine Attainment unto Wisdom.

Zχ

DE MODO QUO HANC EPISTOLAM SCRIPSI

HERE IS NOT ONE WORD IN THIS LETTER that is not writ with mine own Hand and Style, slowly and heedfully (as is contrary with my Custom), being the Fruit of the Tree of my Meditation, well-ripened by the Sun of mine Illumination. With much Toil have I done this, being oftentimes seated without Motion save of the Hands, while Earth rolled in Shadow from Twilight unto Twilight, so that my Body became cold and rigid, even as is a Corpse. Also, in the Intervals of this Scripture, have I been given to Contemplation and to Works of High Magick, notably the Mass of the Holy Ghost, in the Concentration of my Will to impart this Wisdom unto thee, and to reveal the Mysteries of Truth. Now of all these this is the Root, that Truth is not fixed with the Rigour of Death, but vital with Lust of Change, and enflamed with the Love of its Opposite. Thus even Falsehood is not alien to Truth, for the Perfection of Nature comprehendeth All. But all these Things are written in *The Book of the Law*, after which do I limp painfully, afar off, upon the poor Crutch of mine Understanding of its Word; yea, I am well assured that in that Book are writ all Things soever; but we, being mostly without Wit, are not able to distinguish them. For the Stature of Aiwass is beyond our Measure, seeing that He was able to comprehend the whole Mystery of Nuit and of Hadit, and yet to declare Their Message in the Language of Men.

Zψ

DE SAPIENTIA ET STULTITIA

MY SON, IN THIS THE COLOPHON OF MINE Epistle will I recall the Title and Superscription thereof; that is, *The Book of Wisdom or Folly*. I proclaim Blessing and Worship unto Nuit Our Lady and Her Lord Hadit, for the Miracle of the Anatomy of the Child Ra-Hoor-Khuit, as it is shewed in the Design *Minutum Mundum*, the Tree of Life. For though Wisdom be the Second Emanation of His Essence, there is a Path to separate and to join them, the Reference thereof being Aleph, that is One indeed, but also an Hundred and Eleven in his full Orthography; to signify the Most Holy Trinity, and by Metathesis it is Thick Darkness, and Sudden Death. This is also the Number of AUM, which is AMOUN, and the Root-Sound of OMNE, or, in Greek, PAN, and it is a Number of the Sun. Yet is the Atu of Thoth that correspondeth thereunto marked with ZERO, and its Name is MAT, whereof I have spoken formerly, and its Image is The Fool. O my Son, gather thou all these Limbs together into one Body, and breathe upon it with thy Spirit, that it may live; then do thou embrace it with Lust of thy Manhood, and go in unto it, and know it; so shall ye be One Flesh. Now at last in the Reinforcement and Ecstasy of this Consummation thou shalt wit by what Inspiration thou didst choose thy Name in the Gnosis, I mean PARZIVAL, "der reine Thor," the True Knight that won Kingship in Monsalvat, and made whole the Wound of Amfortas, and ordered Kundry to Right Service, and regained the Lance, and revived the Miracle of the Sangraal; yea, also upon himself did he accomplish his Work in the End: "Höchsten Heiles Wunder! Erlösung dem Erlöser!" This is the last Word of the Song that thine Uncle Richard Wagner made for Worship of this Mystery. Understand thou this, o my Son, as I take Leave of thee in this Epistle, that the Summit of Wisdom is the Opening of the Way that leadeth unto the Crown and Essence of all, to the Soul of the Child Horus, the Lord of the Æon. This Way is the Path of the Pure Fool.

Ζω

DE ORACULO SUMMO

ND WHO IS THIS PURE FOOL? LO, IN THE Sagas of old Time, Legend of Scald, of Bard, of Druid, cometh he not in Green like Spring? O thou Great Fool, thou Water that art Air, in whom all Complex is resolved! Yea, Thou in ragged Raiment, with the Staff of Priapus and the Wineskin! Thou standest up on the Crocodile like Hoor-pa-Kraat; and the Great Cat leapeth upon Thee! Yea, and more also, I have known Thee who Thou art, Bacchus Diphues, none and two, in thy Name IAO! Now at the End of all do I come to the Being of Thee, beyond By-coming, and I cry aloud My Word, as it was given unto Man by thine Uncle Alcofribas Nasier, the Oracle of the Bottle of BACBUC, and this Word is TRINC.

But in the antient right Spelling this is TRINU whereof the Number is the Number of the Name of Me thy Father! to wit, Six Hundred and Three Score and Six.

Love is the law, love under will.

666

An. XIV
☉ in ♈
☽ in ♈

INDEX

General

Technical

Liber Legis

Chapter One

Chapter Two

Chapter Three

This
edition of
Liber א vel CXI
The Book of Wisdom or Folly
was designed by Hymenaeus Beta in
Lanston Monotype Giampa Caslon No. 227
and Goudy No. 30, with Goudy Decorative Initial Capitals